The PROMETHEUS FRONTIER

... to begin the world over again.

written and illustrated by
Kevin Osborne

Editing and design by
Alex Bleier
alexbleiertech@gmail.com

Copyright © 2021 Kevin Osborne
All rights reserved.

This is a work of fiction. Names, characters, organizations, places, events, buildings, incidents are either products of the author's imagination or are used fictitiously. Likewise, any output of the human intellect in this novel, such as philosophic principles, statements, or viewpoints, are either products of the author's imagination or used fictitiously.

The Prometheus Frontier Copyright © 2021 Kevin Osborne

Cover painting Copyright © 2021 Kevin Osborne

All rights reserved. No part of this publication may be reproduced, stored in a retrieval system, or transmitted, in any form, or by any means, electronic, mechanical, photocopying, recording or otherwise, without the prior written consent of the author.

First Edition Published by Mutekikon Publications
Editor: Alex Bleier (v5) 2-16-2023
Contact: alexbleiertech@gmail.com

Also available in Kindle format

To a vision: the island of Arête

PROLOGUE

INTERSTELLAR DUST TO VOLCANIC ISLANDS

And the great goddess Gaia gives birth to many offspring. Among them are the demigods known as Titans who do so much to build her legacy and ensure its permanence in the cosmic drama. But one of these Titans is the defiant Prometheus who audaciously creates thinking beings. These are new and unique creatures that on the vast template of time and by virtue of their capacity to reason become more powerful than all others. Gaia is furious and envious. She sees that she is upstaged and forever after wages war against these thinking beings—Prometheus's legacy.

From an unknown drama by Aeschylus, lost to history until its papyrus is found in the cave of a remote island in the Mediterranean Sea. Its title: *Gaia's War*.

From the beginning, planet Earth had water—immense quantities of water.

Prologue

This is understandable, for throughout the universe, hydrogen is the most common element, with oxygen not far behind. Because each is highly reactive and bonds readily, boundless stretches of interstellar dust and gas contain water in the form of ice. Indeed, ice is the most abundant solid object. Not surprisingly then, when this dust and gas coalesce to form solar systems, certain planets and moons—if conditions of pressure, temperature, and gravity are fortuitous—trap huge masses of water beneath their mantles. Earth, due in large measure to size and distance from its sun, was one of those planets. And so, it joined the other water-blessed planets and moons in the universe—they would be countless—all offspring of the eternally-repeating cosmic drama of stellar evolution.

After planet Earth came into being, a different form of evolution began. A volatile molten core seethed beneath her massive reservoirs of captured water; for more than half a billion years, volcanic eruptions broke through her crust and spewed superheated gasses high into the primordial atmosphere. Water vapor was one of those gasses. When it cooled, it condensed into rain, and the rain inundated the planet with water. Eventually, it reached a depth of more than two miles over her entire surface. Temperature and pressure maintained the water in its liquid state; gravity prevented it from escaping into space.

This was a blessing, for the water soothed Mother Earth, slaking her passion for violence until finally there was the relative quiet of a breathless potentiality. A new planet, blanketed by water, was now ready to define herself. Thales of Miletus, philosopher-scientist of Ancient Greece, could he have witnessed it, would have been taken by it all. He it was who identified water as the originating principle of everything else, as if he had somehow divined the above drama.

Subsequent acts in the drama confirmed his principle. Lightning bolts, striking the rich chemical soup of ancient ocean water, triggered the creation of a new *stuff*. This stuff was a

Prologue

fusion of carbon and hydrogen and other elements. The stuff was animate matter, *living* matter. This is matter that could replicate itself, the never-seen-before complexity of which would become an inextricable part of Earth's history.

Earth's animated matter was exclusively microbial for an unimaginable span of time. It was billions of years before the plants and animals evolved. But microbes had paved the way for them with atmospheric oxygen, that vital product of one microbe in particular, photosynthetic cyanobacteria. Then, as if in full circle, all life, to this day, fundamentally depends on microbes to function, survive, and thrive.

Earth's evolution was not smooth. Although relentless, it was marked by fits and starts, extinctions and re-starts. Some were cataclysmic, and the planet's ever-changing geology was a sweeping canvas for it all. But one portion of the canvas was especially significant. Cooler parts of the planet's crust were pulled downwards into the molten lower mantle, and this weakened the surrounding crust. Many repetitions led to plate-like boundaries that gradually formed giant tectonics adrift on a viscous lower layer. Later, these evolved into separate land masses that eventually merged, before breaking apart again. This happened more than once in the planet's four and a half billion years. Evidence suggests that the most recent was three hundred million years ago and was the supercontinent scientists call *Pangaia—Pan* for *"All"* and *Gaia* for *"Earth."* Pangaia's eventual breakup yielded today's continents and demarcated Earth's various oceans and seas.

One of these oceans is the Atlantic, and a small part of the Atlantic is the Caribbean Sea. This sea is a million square miles of such breathtaking beauty, that it easily rivals that of the slightly smaller Mediterranean Sea. Its depths bottom out on the Caribbean plate situated between the much larger ones of North and South America. Many islands, primarily volcanic, formed in

Prologue

the Caribbean Sea, products of tectonic plate movement—processes that are still at work today.

Over the centuries, European countries colonized these islands and vied for dominance. War, slavery, and imported pathogens decimated native populations, but slaves imported from Africa replaced them. Because the climate was ideal, the sugar trade prevailed, and the islands became known as Sugar Islands.

But this name disguised a curse. The sugar trade was based on a savage and inhuman scourge—slavery.

Slavery is gone, but the islands remain in the stultifying grip of coercion, albeit of a different stripe. Paternal authoritarian governments keep these lush lands stopped in time—still. The islands could be hugely prosperous, but they are not. Instead, they are typically marked by various levels of stagnation and, in some cases, outright impoverishment.

Except for a rare exception ...

———

Table of Contents

PROLOGUE i
STOWAWAYS 1
ORIBEL 4
PERPETUAL FLAME 11
PANGAIA 20
VENTANA 27
MAREK 38
LENORE 47
VINDAUGE 55
DECLARATION 64
NEURON 71
IN OUR POWER 80
PAINE 88
RANKL'S FOLLY 94
PRIORITIES 102
THE IMMORTALS 115
DRAGON & HELIX 126
WARRIORS OF THE MIND 138
INAUGURATION 148
EUDAIMONIA 159
CRISIS 171
UNLIMITED FUTURE 186
EPILOGUE 189
Acknowledgements 196

STOWAWAYS

The ship rolled over long swells of ocean under a luminous gray sky. A great hurricane was raging more than 250 miles to starboard, and the air was wet with it, and agitated—even at this distance. Sprays of water were ripped from the waves and flung into the growing tropical light—bursts of unbridled freedom. There was a wild beauty to it all, to which the ship was utterly oblivious.

Stowaways

Deep below deck, inside one of its containers, stowaways huddled. They were a young man and woman, recently married, and five days ago, they had committed themselves to this voluntary entombment, along with an aunt and uncle. Women's apparel filled the twenty-foot-long chamber, a soft cargo that was able to yield space to four bodies with meager possessions, though with great reluctance. Except for the aunt, whose entire work life had been with a cigar maker, all in the family had labored in the sweat shops of their island's garment industry. That was their common connection to this particular ship—and container.

Perhaps it also explained their folly. Once locked inside this tomb, they found that they were effectively buried alive. They were barely able to move and were in total darkness except for a few flashlights without spare batteries. Not a one of the four stowaways spoke of the dark claustrophobia which was little better than the impoverishment of the life they were fleeing—or of the abject terror that consumed them. It was not their way to complain. Their way was to pull together, each a source of support for the others.

Soon, however, the aunt succumbed to the oppressive heat and, the next day, the uncle. The family had been assured by their contact that the container would be above deck, but he was not speaking the truth. There was no way he could have known that. With hand drill and hacksaw, the stowaways had been able to cut vents in the reinforced walls of the container. This gave them air to breathe, but it was without the wind chill and air circulation that they would have had above deck. The heat in the ship's cargo hold was suffocating, and because dry-goods containers do not require temperature control, their battle, from day one, had been a losing one.

On this the fifth day, the two survivors were squatting on the makeshift bed that all of them had once shared. They faced each other and held hands to balance themselves against the nauseating motion of the ship. In their exhaustion, they leaned forward and their foreheads touched. Their relatives were now sealed within plastic sheets that had once been garment protection. And that dreadful task had physically and emotionally depleted them. Finally, the young woman spoke. "We are on our last water bottle, my husband, and our last flashlight is nearly spent. I feel so weak. I fear for us."

"I know, my Livia, but remember our old life. We want so much more than that. Think of our new island . . . a most excellent place . . . where we can grow . . . and thrive. Rest now."

Still holding hands, they lowered their bodies.

The next day, the ship's rolling had lessened. Lying on their backs now, the couple could hear the beating of the diesel engines, the heart of the beast whose belly they were in. The young man spoke into the darkness. "I should not have trusted that man. He took our money and deceived us. We were supposed to be safe. I have failed you, my wife, and I have failed our family."

She did not answer. But then, "You did not fail us, husband. Our dream island . . . filled with hope . . ." and her voice trailed off. Until finally, she spoke, "It was worth it, my Angel. Yes, it *is* worth it, Angel Ramos."

He was beyond hearing, and she feared it was too late—for both of them. But had there been light, she would have seen the trace of a smile remaining in the corners of his mouth. He was far away now, dreaming of another place, a place of unlimited opportunity—and unbridled freedom. It was a place of excellence—unsurpassed excellence.

ORIBEL

Marek Rankl could not remember a time he did not love islands. At this very moment, in the forty-second year of his life, his yacht *Oribel* was approaching a small Caribbean island that he wanted to make his own. He thought of the huge number of islands in the world. Most of them originated from oceanic volcanoes, and the rest were offspring of continental shelves. More than ten percent of the world's population lived on islands. From a lifetime of studying islands, Marek Rankl knew this.

But his main interest was in a special subset of islands, the *tropical* ones. Tens of thousands of them, each twelve or more acres, populated the world's oceans. It was a tropical island of one thousand acres that had been taking shape for the past half hour, as he watched from his yacht's bridge. He said to his captain, "Dial it back a bit, Armando. I want to approach slowly and circle it before we land." The island was roughly trapezoidal in shape, and they were approaching it from the southwest.

As the island drew closer, its volcanic mountain, long dormant, dominated their view. It rose to over seven hundred feet, on the island's southern coast. This coast, stretching for a mile and a half, was the longest side of the trapezoid. The Oribel then went to port to start a clockwise circuit up the western coastline.

Lush tropical vegetation enveloped the island in green. Low cliffs, varying in height, edged its circumference, girding the island against the relentless onslaught of the sea. The Oribel circled the northern tip and progressed south, down the eastern coast. At its mid-point, Rankl was struck by what he saw and said, "Let's hold it here, Armando."

Oribel

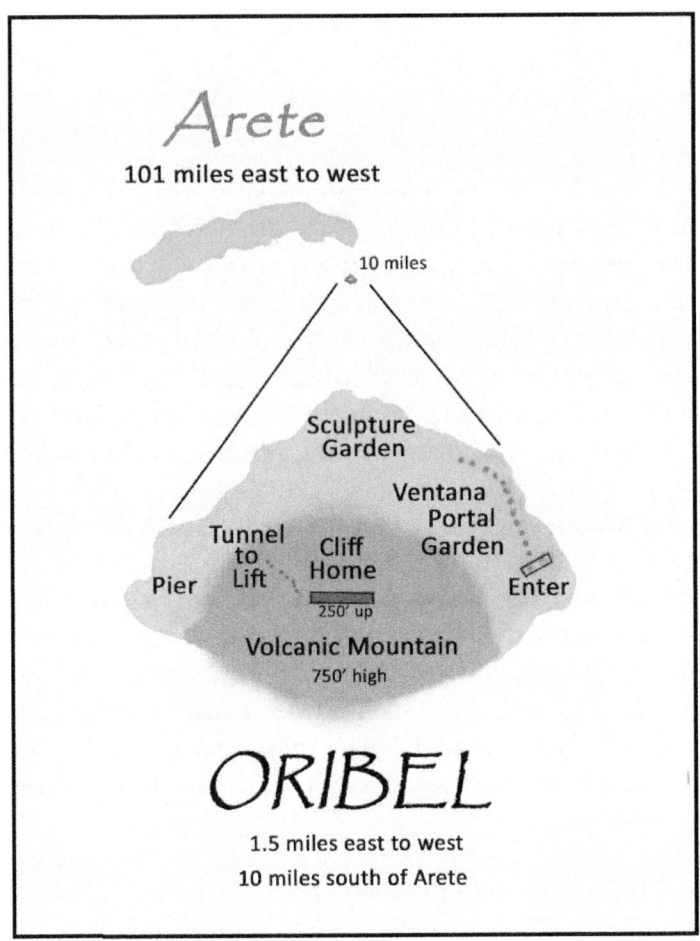

The north face of the mountain had come into view, and a third of the way up, a cliff had been hewn—sculpted—out of the lava rock. This cliff became a long balcony for an excavated dwelling behind it, all of it made possible by the materials and heavy equipment that had been air-lifted onto the island for that purpose. Mango trees, growing directly above, provided shade, and continuous horizontal windows ran its entire length. During the day, the dwelling was visible mainly by the light reflected off the glass. It was a subtle presence, a natural part of the small mountain.

Oribel

Marek Rankl spoke again. "That balcony, looking to the northern end of the island, reminds me of the bridge we are on here in the Oribel. I think we have the name of our small island, old friend."

"Oribel."

"Yes. Golden Beauty."

"Perfecta."

Having completed their circuit, they headed for the pier on the south western coast. The island sloped down to it, for the cliff was lower at this point. An old man was waiting, and Rankl recognized Jorge Besosa, the owner of the island, the man he had come to see. After introductions, they headed up an incline for the lift to his home. Armando was securing the Oribel, and Besosa called back, "Join us when you finish, Capitán Rojas."

Their conversation paused while Rankl pondered the implications of what his host had just said. They were sitting in the long living room of the dwelling, looking across the island toced the Caribbean Sea and the much larger island to the north. Spacious windows ran the full length of the room and framed a medley of translucent blues and greens. Breakers approached and lost themselves against the cliffs, below their line of sight.

White longtails crisscrossed in the sky overhead, and Marek learned from his host that he had introduced this tern species to the island many years earlier, from elsewhere in the Caribbean. It had flourished.

For a full minute, the only sound was the ice cubes in their glasses. Then Besosa broke the silence. "Yes, my friend, I know what you are thinking, now that you have heard my story. What you have learned, is known to only a few. And now you have a

Oribel

decision to make, bigger than the one you came here to talk about today."

Jorge Besosa had been born and raised on the much larger island ten miles to the north. As a youth, he became enamored with Caribbean revolutionaries, above all, the famed Brazilian Marxist, Chan Chan Morales. Morales was a flamboyant guerilla leader and skilled propagandist educated in leftist ideology. The young Besosa devoured all he could find on him, and his parents encouraged their son in his studies. The Besosa family had controlled the island for more than a century, and when the time came for college, they sent Jorge to London's renowned Karl Marx Institute. He excelled there.

When he took over the reins of government from his father, Jorge Besosa was thoroughly imbued with socialist ideology. His education reinforced what his father had taught him as a youth—that capitalism is a system of cutthroat competition, a system in which one swims with the sharks or gets eaten; that capitalism is a system of class struggle where the wealthy dominate and control poor starving workers; that because socialism addresses these ills, the fact that, under it, the lives of the people belong to the state—in this case the Besosa regime—was, they were told, a small price to pay.

Early in the Besosa era, the island had gained its independence and had become a sovereign nation. But it was already largely impoverished by a history of coercion, corruption, destructive agricultural practices, and abysmal stewardship of its resources and infrastructure.

After Jorge's ascension to power, however, there was improvement. In college, when he had studied *Das Capital,* he noted Marx's statement in the preface that, historically, the productive superiority of a market economy was indisputable. And so, during his years of study abroad, he read widely in the extensive literature of free enterprise. He was greatly taken by the work of a Chilean economist, Fernando de Gama, with his emphasis on the vital importance of property rights. In addition, he studied the Austrian and Chicago schools of economics.

He also studied the history of the Aegean and became fascinated with Greece's golden age from five hundred to three hundred BC. He resolved to develop his island and to make it a great power in the Caribbean, in short, a place of excellence. And thus, he renamed it *Arête,* Greek for excellence, or virtue.

When Jorge Besosa assumed control, he sought to promote market forces, the profit motive, and property rights. Improvement was rapid in many sectors of his island's economy. And as a result, it became a haven for Caribbean refugees fleeing the impoverishment of their islands.

A family by the name of Ramos was among them, who created and then managed a new immigration program for Arête. It became well known, and Jorge Besosa, very much the driver of it all, was lauded in the Caribbean as a youthful idealist.

Oribel

But the improvements did not last. To his dismay, Besosa's mixed economy of market forces and state controls inexorably trended to nearly complete government control. His ministers found the reins of power hard to surrender. For every setback, they simply concluded that more government intervention was needed. That meant less freedom, and Jorge Besosa invariably signed off on it. Gradually, freedom was lost on Arête.

In recent years, an intensified period of calamities had beset the island. Hurricanes occurred regularly, with devastating impact on infrastructure. Outbreaks of cholera and other diseases often followed. Invariably, global climate change was seen as the culprit, and an underlying despair of the situation ever improving sapped the island's energy.

High level government bureaucrats began to abscond with what wealth they could. Lower-level bureaucrats, too, each of them a looter in his own way, further depleted what scant island resources remained.

Seeing what was happening and helpless to do anything about it, the population fled except for the stubborn few who struggled on. Most of these owned their own homes and had a bare subsistence existence, farming or running small businesses.

The remaining few were subcontractors taking in simple work from other islands, making cigars or hand stitching colorful Caribbean accents onto garments—such as those in the Ramos's container ship years earlier. They were a middle class, of sorts. But, gradually, they became more impoverished, and, as Arête Island limped along in this state, its population dwindled.

———

By the end of his story, Jorge Besosa's creased face was etched with sadness. He looked at Rankl and saw that his final words had touched a nerve. He had no way of knowing that his guest already knew his island's history. Nor did he know that Armando Rojas had made Rankl aware of facts not commonly known—important facts. Watching his guest, Besosa could only ask himself: Is this the man to give my Arête a new life—a man for whom it is not too late? Is this why my final words have him sitting in stunned silence?

"My remaining ministers," Jorge had admitted to his guest, "each of them basically an honest man, is looking to get out of the whole cursed thing. Like me, Señor Rankl ... like me, they are very old and very, very tired—*agotado*."

PERPETUAL FLAME

The time was early in the third millennium, and the century, now in its fourth quarter, was mature. A Caribbean island was the place; it was known as Arête.

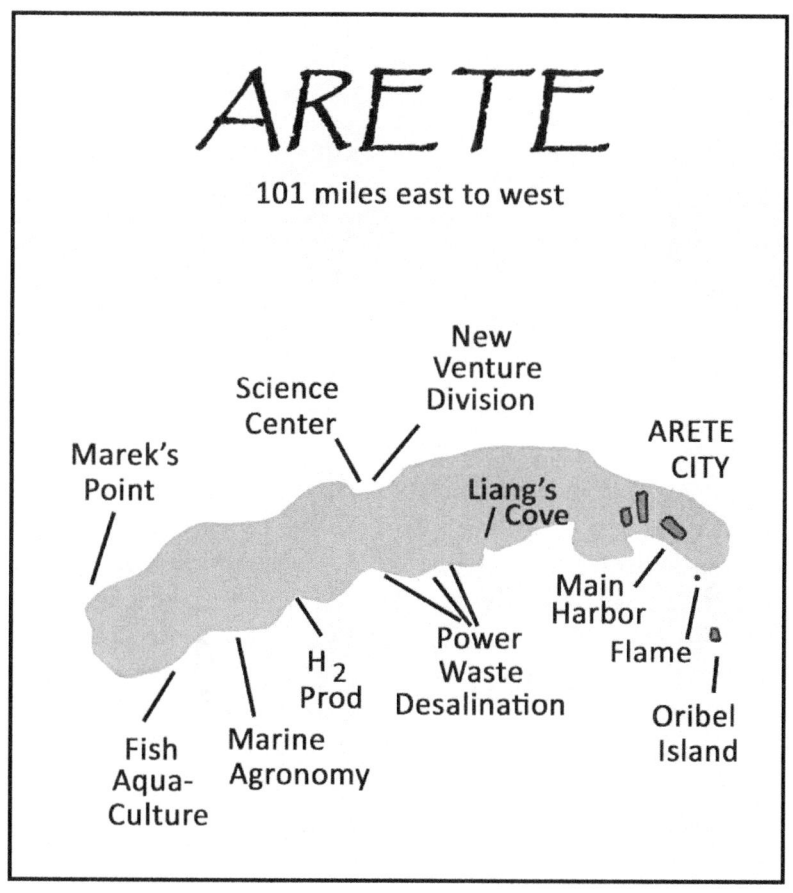

Arête City, its capital, was on the eastern tip of the island. Approaching it from the south, one was greeted by a youthful skyline.

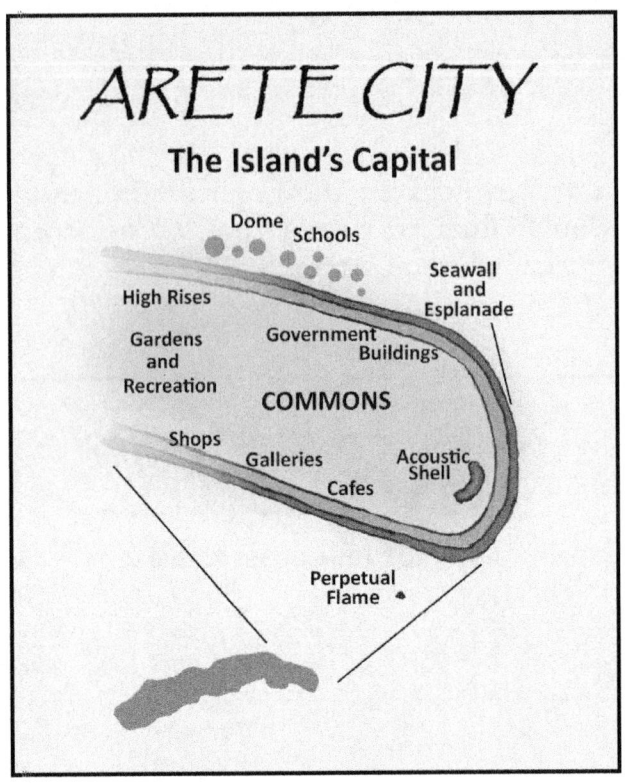

Also, by a seawall, a major infrastructure project completed five years earlier. It started several miles to the west, where a deep coastal indentation formed Arête's largest natural harbor. The coastline connecting this harbor to the island's eastern tip was a relatively smooth one, vulnerable to ocean forces—hence the seawall. From start to finish, the wall was nearly ten miles long, for after curving around the island's tip, it continued west for a few more miles before ending.

From that point Arête continued for another ninety-five miles. Overall, the island described a long curving arc in the Caribbean

Perpetual Flame

Sea, with a mean distance north to south of roughly eleven miles. Much of its coastline was indented, and this blessed it with a number of bays.

The seawall embracing the capital city made possible a generous avenue—an esplanade. Along its curve, on the eastern tip of the island, there stood a concert stage. The exterior wall of its large acoustic shell was on the edge of the esplanade, and a long flagpole rose up from the shell's roof.

The stage looked out onto a spacious commons of tropical foliage, gardens, and meadows. Numerous paved paths—edged by composite benches of coral, granite, and driftwood—had been bringing Arêteans in all morning. It was a special day.

Certain journalists had been watching Arête for a decade, ever since renowned scientist and industrialist, Marek Rankl, had purchased it. But typically, they dismissed the island. As a new venture, they regarded it as another blue-sky dream, which would go nowhere.

It was little surprise then, that the pending event attracted scant attention. Two outside writers were present, however, from the City Herald of New York, a weekly magazine of ideas. They watched from the far end of the commons, away from the stage. From here they could take it all in, as could the spectators on the balconies of the nearby high rises.

Many people were standing in groups, quietly conversing. Others were sitting on the benches or relaxing on the ground. For the large open area in front of the stage, some people brought their own chairs, but they were the exception. Children of all ages and their parents were on blankets or colorful beach towels.

Regardless of age, even the youngest were calm, as if sensing the importance of the day.

The prevailing mood was not lost on the two visitors. "Whatever we might think," noted one of them from the side of his mouth, "something important is in the air." He was a paunchy man wearing a garish floral shirt and a straw hat. His colleague glanced at him and saw the trace of a sneer still on his lips, a residue of the sarcasm she detested.

"I agree about something important being in the air but not with what you'd consider that *something* to be," she said. He looked her way, but she had forgotten he existed. A turquoise headband held back her shoulder-length, deep-bronze hair, and her eyes were focused on a large flag in the distance. It was high above the acoustic shell. The flag was a golden flame on a rich blue background, and it was ablaze in the morning sun. It's a real flame, the woman said to herself, as she watched it trembling in the breeze.

On stage, a conductor's podium had been moved close to the edge and rotated to face the audience. Finally, the commons went silent as men and women, one by one, entered from stage rear and took the chairs awaiting them. They were to one side and slightly back from the podium. When they were seated, some two dozen of them, a final figure appeared and made his way forward. Everyone on stage and out in the commons stood. The man carried himself with relaxed authority. His name was Marek Rankl.

His eyes swept the audience. He paused, and his face lit with a smile. Then he spoke. "Ladies and gentlemen, and children of Arête, this morning, all of us, by virtue of our presence on this island, are witness to, and part of, a unique moment in human history.

Perpetual Flame

"Today we inaugurate the Prometheus Frontier's first sovereign nation—Arête.

"Our founders are before you on this stage. And the flag you see high above is *our* flag. Its golden flame, so incandescent in the morning sun, symbolizes the fire of reason which Prometheus, in the ancient Greek myth, stole from the gods and brought to mankind. We have brought the same fire to Arête, an island where human reason and freedom reign supreme."

Our founding documents—our Constitution and the Declaration of Freedom which is both its preamble and animating philosophy—are crystal clear. Our founding documents explicitly, in no uncertain terms, banish physical coercion from all areas of human endeavor, *including*," he stressed, "any area yet to be developed."

He then turned to his right and, with upturned palm, gestured to the sitting men and women. "To execute on this grand quest," he continued, "the Paine Society was chartered ten years ago. Its current members are before you on this stage. Their charter—*to begin the world over again*—is a vision we all share.

"Executing the vision means setting priorities, financing them, managing unintended consequences, and countless other activities, performed superlatively and unceasingly. Execution is the great challenge—for the Paine Society, for all Arêteans. We Arêteans know how to meet challenges and, with reason our guide, and always learning from mistakes, we get ever better at it."

There was a brief pause as Marek Rankl turned his head and pointed upward. "The flame you see in the flag above us," he said, "is our flame of reason and freedom. It burns in the soul of every Arêtean. Now we are going to bring that flame into concrete existence—an actual, *physical* flame.

Perpetual Flame

"From this day forward, through all future generations, eras, and époques, the flame we are about to light will be visible in the offshore waters of Arête City. Neither force of nature nor of man will ever extinguish it. It will be as invincible as the heroic human spirit it symbolizes. It will be the Prometheus Frontier's perpetual flame of reason and freedom."

The crowd stirred and the breeze seemed to quicken as a sweeping applause began and spread across the commons. Everyone was now standing. Children could be seen jumping up and down, unable to contain their energy.

Silence was restored, however, as the stage emptied and the airspace above it took on a subtle shimmering effect. This told the audience that they were about to experience what was colloquially known as an ultra-immersion augmentation. They knew that without any special equipment, other than their five senses, they would be intimately and totally drawn into the next portion of the program. They would not need to budge from where they stood.

It commenced with the low rumble of powerful engines from somewhere under the stage. As the engines slowly ramped up, the audience felt as if their bodies were being drawn inexorably toward the stage. After a minute or so, this feeling trailed off and was followed by the sensation that they had settled into an open craft on the Caribbean Sea. Salt spray filled their nostrils and found its way to their tongues as their eyes told them that they were making for Arête City, small on the horizon. While they looked, they felt the vibrating craft through the soles of their feet, as its engines closed the distance.

A mile from the island, they saw a dark rock structure take shape. Near it, buoys signaled the presence of dangerous reefs.

Perpetual Flame

As the vessel slowed and drew closer, the passengers saw that the structure rose seventy-five feet out of the water. From its top a great flaring funnel, carved from black granite, reached for the sky. It was a modern-day fennel stalk—that makeshift torch in the ancient myth, fashioned by Prometheus to steal the divine fire—the fire that he would then bring to mankind.

As the craft slowed still further, its engines gave way to the roar of crashing waves and the shrieking of gulls. The spectators, now fully immersed in the drama, experienced the sensation of wet skin. Their hands went to their ears to quell the raucous cries of the birds. The roar of the waves intensified and then intensified further as it blended with the visual images—the rock structure, the water exploding against it, the wind-ripped sprays of salt.

Now the vessel was crawling as it drew ever closer to the rocks—and then closer still. All motion in the commons had come to a halt. It was as if everyone, their eyes on the approaching boulders, had stopped breathing. Even the children were riveted in place.

Finally, it happened. A great blue flame burst out of the funnel and into the sky with a muted whoosh, the superheated breath of an enormous exhalation. The scent of ignition wafted over the commons. More than one viewer later reported imagining that a giant hand had brought flint down against the black granite of the torch to bring the flame to life.

No one could remember how long it took, but over the next few minutes, the great flame's color gradually warmed. At the same time, its initial height diminished and widened into large tongues of golden flame, filling the granite funnel. Even in the morning's radiant sunlight, the flame was visible for miles around, waving in the wind and reaching fifty feet into the air.

Finally, the audience realized that the stage had gone silent. But a large golden afterimage remained for long moments above it. Then gradually, it disappeared as well. The stage was empty, and a warm, soothing breeze caressed the commons. Another stage had been set—and lit.

The first visiting journalist immediately left for the airport. Burt Bartle was eager to file his report and be done with the island. In the *Arête Aerolounge*, he slumped into a comfortable chair and considered what he wanted to say. As he sipped his second scotch, he balanced a keypad on his paunch, and his stubby fingers proceeded to tap out the words. He filled his account with colorful detail of what he had witnessed, lacing it with strong doses of his trademark sarcasm. He saved the strongest of them for his concluding remarks.

"Arête Island, as so far developed," he said, "is a monument to the *hubris* of one man: Marek Rankl. A paragon of superciliousness, he thought he was officiating—in his words—over a unique moment in human history. Indeed, he was. Never has this writer witnessed a greater display of human arrogance and folly. The arrogance was palpable; the folly was thinking that weak and depraved human beings can be cut loose from the only thing that keeps them from wreaking havoc on the world and its populations—namely, the coercive chains of government regulation. There is something ironic in the fact that the greatest depravity is that exhibited by Marek Rankl himself, as evidenced by his monumental wealth. Is there any activity more depraved than profit seeking," he asked in conclusion. After a quick check, the report was on its way, and Burt Bartle ordered another drink.

His colleague, Emma Lane, who had been so taken with Arête's flag waving in the morning sun, filed a different report. The City Herald of New York had a tradition of featuring both sides of a story. Its editor knew she would get contrasting views from her two writers. When she received Emma Lane's report, a few hours after Bartle's, it was as she expected. Nor was she surprised that

Lane had booked a vacation rental for an exploratory week on Arête.

"Today, an otherwise unremarkable Caribbean island," Lane opened, "going by the name, Arête, Greek for excellence or virtue, has made an entirely remarkable proclamation. It has proclaimed that the island nation of Arête is a haven where initiated physical coercion has no place. Constitutional law prohibits it—from any source, whether government or private. The only physical force permitted to the government is retaliatory force, and only against those who have already initiated physical coercion or threatened to do so."

She then proceeded to describe the spectacular lighting of the flame. Finally, she closed her account where it had to close. "After the flame was lit," she wrote, "Arêteans remained in place, as if too stunned to move. But at length, they resumed their lives. Most of them left the commons of Arête City—I myself was among them—and crossed the esplanade to the top edge of the seawall. There we stood in silence as our gaze was pulled over the water to a golden flame one mile away—never to be extinguished.

"Ever to be known as the *Perpetual Flame of Reason and Freedom.*"

PANGAIA

The woman exited the condominium complex and walked out into the salt air. Turning right, she headed north on the elevated plaza. At the end, she heard the traffic hissing along the river drive three stories below, before entering the relative quiet of a waiting elevator pod.

A short distance behind, a personal guard had been shadowing her. He joined her in the pod, and the doors closed. It dropped and moved laterally, then dropped again, before opening onto a walkway to a nearby water shuttle. Boarding it, she made for the forward railing, as her guard let the distance between them grow again, all the time watching the other passengers, without watching them.

She was a slender presence, elderly, and smartly dressed. Her air was slightly imperious. The other commuters, some of them residents of her condominium complex, stared in mild annoyance. They knew she enjoyed the fact that the shuttle's captain had kept them waiting for her to arrive.

As the vessel moved off, she leaned against the rail and craned her head back to take in the rectangular glass façade of the building she had just exited. For more than a century, its forty stories had served as the administration building of One World. But the One World organization had again taken on a new identity. It was now known as *Pangaia*—Greek for *All Earth*. Its

Pangaia

location was different as well. Pangaia had been granted sovereignty over a 170-acre island in New York harbor. The island, very close to the tip of New York City's borough of Manhattan, became the site of Pangaia's world headquarters. It was the woman's destination this morning.

Directly above, a seagull hung on the breeze. Then, dipping a wing, it was swept away. The water shuttle, as if on cue, started down river, following the eastern edge of Manhattan Island and the city that had once been the financial capital of the world.

The woman ordinarily would have used the speedier air vehicle service down to Manhattan's southern tip and then transferred to a water shuttle for the short hop to Pangaia Island. But on days with weighty concerns, like this one, she preferred the open air and leisurely pace of the shuttle for the entire trip. It afforded her time to clear her head.

The sun was warm on her back, and the vessel passed under three aged bridges before entering the city's main harbor. To starboard, she could see the pale green of the Statue of Liberty. Its right arm was still aloft, but it no longer held a torch into the sky. The arm now ended at the elbow, the point at which vandals had focused their laser weapons years earlier. It was the end of a fiction, she said to herself, as she looked at it. The iconic figure had not been repaired.

Then she remembered another torch, a real one, an actual burning flame more than 2000 miles to the south. The thought of it was always a nasty intrusion, but especially today. That other torch was intimately related, she knew, to the address she would be making this afternoon.

But Pangaia Island was drawing closer. As she watched it grow in size, she felt a familiar sense of power. She was Pangaia's General Secretary.

Pangaia

Pangaia's buildings varied in footprint, but they were all the same height. None of them was more than three stories, as if anything higher would have been an affront to the others. Then, to underscore the uniformity, each building had the same neutral gray sheen.

Paved walkways at ground level connected the buildings, and a grand walkway circled the entire island. A fleet of battery-powered pods handled the daily flow of commuters and tourists. Each wheeled pod, voice activated, could handle a dozen or more passengers, and the island's control center kept everything flowing without mishap. There was no other vehicle traffic on the island.

Leaving the dock area, the woman entered a small personal pod to her destination, as her personal guard set off on foot for his office in a nearby building. Once his charge was on Pangaia Island, the island's security system took over.

As she entered her headquarters building, she took in the familiar surroundings. A spacious, high-ceilinged chamber welcomed the many daily visitors. At this moment, however, it was still an hour before opening.

The chamber contained a profusion of sitting areas equipped with expanded-reality headsets to take visitors to any realm they wished. Hi-res displays were ubiquitous, linked to an endless stream of news, entertainment and social networks. A constant array of lively documentaries dealt with causes championed by Pangaia: climate change, environmental decline, wealth disparity, and many other evils it attributed to the existence of free enterprise in the world. Everything about this building was international in scope, including the fact, that a long passageway connected its entry chamber to a spacious International Assembly Hall.

Pangaia

Aerial drobots hovered here and there, ready to answer questions or take orders for the always-complimentary refreshments. The Pangaia Panini was a favorite. Surveys confirmed that the stimulation-laden experience of the building strongly imprinted itself on young visitors and often led them to Pangaia-related careers later—exactly the effect intended.

To the left, the walls contained large back-lit images of Pangaia, streaming in continuous loops. There were exterior views of buildings and the landscaping between them. Other views captured the interiors of conference centers, religious facilities, and media rooms.

There was an over-sized panel on which continually looping images slowly morphed, each one into the next, so as to accentuate their basic similarities. This had a hypnotic effect on viewers and especially delighted children. Ancient Pangaia morphed into Earth's current continents and then slowly back to the original supercontinent before ending with a large photo of Pangaia Island in New York harbor. Throughout these transitions, the similarities in shape were vivid.

Other morph transitions made clear that the main structures on the island delineated the seven main regions of modern-day Earth: North America, South America, Africa, Eurasia, Middle East, South China Sea, and Oceana.

To the right, an alcove twenty-five feet wide curved inward to a depth of four feet. At the midpoint, there was a large oil painting. Its plate announced *Herbert Henry, Founder of Pangaia*. The portrait depicted a robust man in navy blue suit and a tie festooned with small gold symbols, each in the shape of Pangaia. His chin tilted slightly upward, suggesting the pose of a visionary, which was how he had always fancied himself.

Pangaia

A burst of white hair stood out on the square block of his head, as did his outsized ears. Otherwise, his features were quite ordinary. During his long life, he had been more remembered for his written and spoken words than his personal appearance. In the portrait, he was benignly gazing to his left, as if he were looking at the words etched into the curving wall—*his* words. The heading at the top read, *The Social Philosophy of Pangaia*, and his eyes were on Principle One. The alcove was an installation, and an authoritative male voice—*his*—could be heard softly enunciating the words at spaced intervals.

> Only the Group is real;
> individuals are like cells of the human body;
> they have reality only as members of a Group.

The other side of the alcove contained smaller images of general secretaries, starting with the first. The last of them was larger, however, nearly the same size as the founder's portrait, next to which it hung. This was the current secretary general, a youthful Galea Magre, at the start of her tenure, decades ago. The image returned her gaze as she entered her office behind the alcove, a considerably older woman with pulled-back silver hair, taut skin over high cheekbones, and a small, pursed mouth, defined by dark lip gloss.

The wall behind her desk displayed her Bachelor of Science in Economics and Master of Science in Cultural Anthropology. Both had been awarded by MSMS, the Manhattan School of Marxist Studies.

There was a framed reproduction of a Forthright Magazine cover. It featured her head and the caption, The World's Most Influential Woman. Off to one side of her desk, there were two wooden pedestals. The first held Herbert Henry's masterwork, *Pangaia: Icon of Collectivism;* the second held Magre's biography, *Herbert Henry: Magisterial Inspiration of Pangaia*.

Pangaia

Secretary General Magre leaned forward in her chair and voiced an order. The opposite wall immediately displayed several paragraphs of text that she then began to voice edit. It was the final touches to what she wanted to cover that day in Pangaia's Grand Assembly Hall.

> Seventy-five years ago, a new island nation was founded 2000 miles south of Pangaia headquarters. This was in the Caribbean Sea. The island, whose name is Arête, defiantly stands for everything to which Pangaia is opposed. Arête champions individualism in a world where any enlightened nation knows the individual is a fiction.
>
> Arête champions individual achievement, ownership, and private property. But, as our great founder Herbert Henry taught us, the fruits of the earth belong to us all, and the earth itself belongs to nobody. The general will, expressed by one great collective body, Pangaia, needs to rule in order to enforce equitable distribution.
>
> Pangaia champions cooperation and sharing between all nations. Arête defiantly drains the world's best minds from those nations most in need of those minds.
>
> Arête champions freedom when the entire world knows that human nature is innately weak—even depraved. History has always taught us that to leave humans free to pursue their own interests is to doom planet Earth: its human populations are pillaged at the same time its climate, natural resources, oceans, and species diversity are steadily destroyed.

General Secretary Magre's list continued and at the end of it, she sat pondering the final affront. Arête never sought recognition by Pangaia, and certainly not membership. She sat

Pangaia

in her chair, in the grip of a deep loathing—a loathing for that island to the south and the flaming torch in its offshore waters.

And everything that that torch represented.

―――

VENTANA

The young man stood at the entrance to a garden, a sizeable clearing that had been cut out of the lush vegetation. This was on a small Caribbean island with the name of Oribel, a place he had long wanted to visit.

For more than a century, the island had been in the young man's family. He knew little about it except that ownership had started with his great-grandfather, Marek, but that now his uncle Eric and aunt Rhianna made it their home.

The young man was Alek Rankl, and over the years, he had occasionally sought an invitation to the island. Each time, however, he was gently asked to be patient. They would let him know.

During the endless wait, the mystery of Oribel only increased for him. It had become clear that the island was skilled in shielding itself from surveillance. And what little *was* known, had, for the most part, been successfully spun over the years to mislead the curious. Finally, having reached his mid-twenties and having completed a milestone in his education, Alek Rankl heard from his aunt and uncle.

A jet had taken him to within ten miles of Oribel by putting down on the larger island of Arête, to the north. It was shortly after dark, and he quickly transferred to his uncle's private air vehicle. As he settled into the passenger seat, safety harnesses automatically engaged, and the AV lifted vertically 200 feet. It followed the coastline a few miles east, to the lights of Arête City and then banked to starboard over the water.

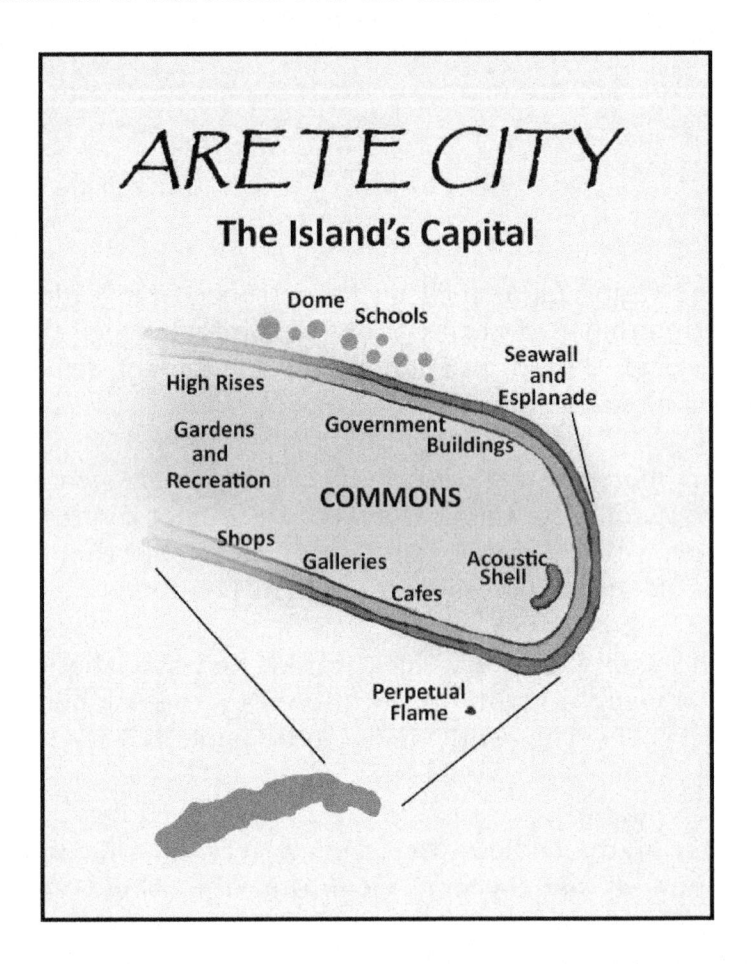

ARETE CITY
The Island's Capital

- Dome
- Schools
- High Rises
- Seawall and Esplanade
- Gardens and Recreation
- Government Buildings
- COMMONS
- Shops
- Galleries
- Acoustic Shell
- Cafes
- Perpetual Flame

They flew south for a mile, slowed to hover mode, and swung back to face the city. The vehicle's hydrogen engines were barely audible as it hung, motionless, in the tropical air. Reaching up from the nearby water, a large golden flame moved languidly, as if waving to them.

Ventana

The older man looked at the slim figure in the other seat. He saw hazel eyes pause on the flame before shifting to the intensely lit coastline. Arête City was the island's capital.

The long esplanade embracing it was a luminous bright band of light from the many cafes, galleries, and shops that lined it. They would remain open at least until midnight. Below the esplanade, fishing boats and pleasure craft, in various shades of white filled the continuous line of piers and marinas edging the seawall. From Alek's distance, however, they were all undefined and simply blended with the bright band of light on the horizon. On the other side of the city, taller structures existed, government buildings and high-rise apartments, but they were too distant to be visible clearly.

Suddenly a rain shower triggered the intense color dots of opening umbrella on the esplanade. The AV moved forward and banked closely near the waving flame, reversing direction again, as it headed for Oribel, ten miles to the south. "You'll be back here in several days," the man said, "after your Ventana orientation."

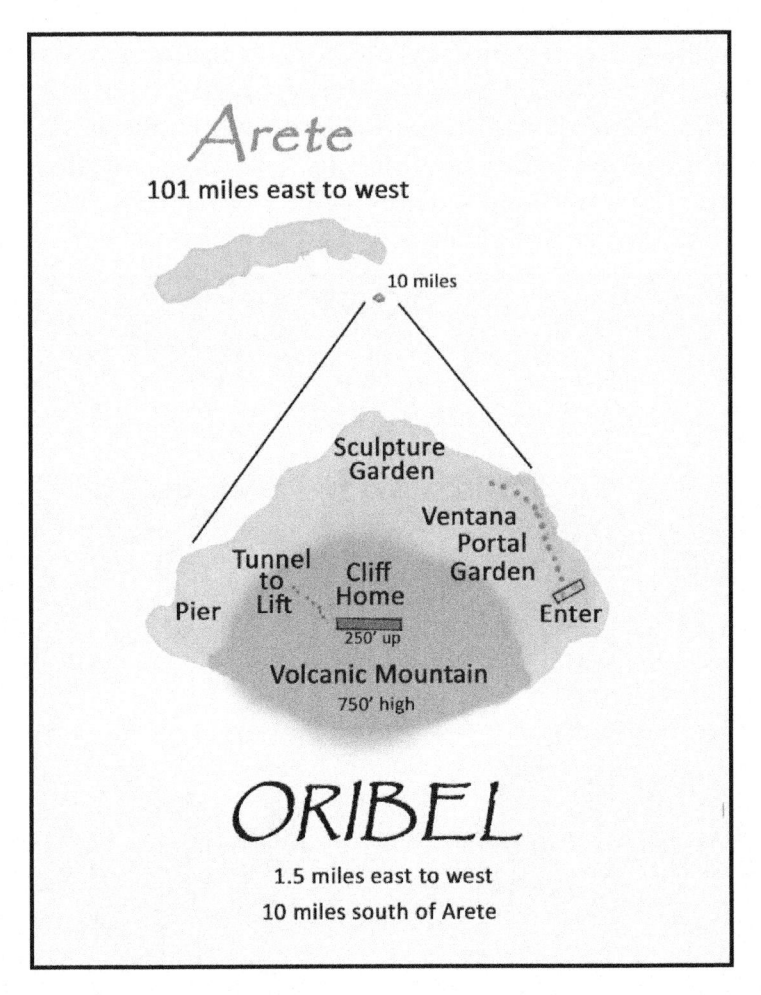

```
Arete
101 miles east to west

                    10 miles

              Sculpture
              Garden
                        Ventana
                        Portal
        Tunnel   Cliff  Garden
        to       Home
  Pier  Lift            Enter
                250' up
          Volcanic Mountain
              750' high

ORIBEL
1.5 miles east to west
10 miles south of Arete
```

He saw the unasked question on his nephew's face and added, "Ventana is a garden of sorts. The map in your room refers to it as a *Garden of Windows*. During the coming week you'll spend time there; it will explain why we kept you waiting so long."

Early the next morning, Alek Rankl found Ventana to be a short walk from the cliff dwelling. Bursts of exotic blooms defined each side of its entrance, and tropical leaves shimmered in a warm breeze. White longtails crisscrossed in the sky overhead.

When Alek stepped into the garden, he saw an outcropping about eight feet high and tapering a bit, as it ran the garden's length. It was parallel to, and slightly in from the island's eastern coast. At the far end, the island opened up to the Caribbean, with Arête a pale gray blue on the horizon.

His eyes were drawn in that direction by a string of metallic portal markers set into the rock outcropping every several feet. Each of them was twelve inches square, five feet from the ground, and marked the location of a holo-lasic portal station. Alek recognized the old but still-versatile technology, once widely used for presentations of all kinds.

The first portal plate read *Welcome,* and he was about to activate it when his Aunt Rhianna appeared. "I see you're about to start," she said, handing him a container of coffee. "Breakfast will be ready in an hour. It's buffet, so just come up when you're ready."

When he started, a virtual headset settled into place on his forehead, perceptible only by the sudden heightened clarity of his visual field. He found himself in the presence of a middle-aged man, every bit as lifelike as an actual person—if anything, even more so. No longer was Alek in a garden on a small Caribbean island. This man was his only reality. His most striking features were a determined mouth and the direct gaze of deeply set grey eyes. His hair was dark and thick—a blessing that one might expect to become gray with time but not thin. He started to speak, and his voice had an engaging intensity.

Ventana

Welcome to Ventana. If you are here in this place, it means you have been watched for a considerable time and judged ready for a vital role—should you choose to accept it. Before this role is revealed to you, however, you will walk a gauntlet, so to speak. It consists of this string of portals, or windows. As you progress through them, you will witness the birth of a vision and the steps to its actualization—its execution.

Specifically, you will see what we had to accomplish to bring this vision into concrete reality and to ensure its success across time.

You are surely wondering why such an elaborate device as this garden is needed. The reasons will become fully clear over the next several days. Paramount among them is the vital need for you to gain, firsthand, a comprehensive understanding of our history. You cannot fully appreciate the importance of your potential role otherwise. If you are here, it means we are confident that you will accept the role we have envisioned for you. Or, if you do not, that the sensitive nature of these portals will not be shared with those who are less than friendly to us. I do not need to tell you that they are many.

So let us begin.

I, Marek Rankl, purchased this fair island from a benevolent dictator by the name of Jorge Besosa and named it after my yacht, Oribel, the vessel that first took me here. Oribel Island and the much larger Arête, also purchased not long after, are ten miles from each other. As for me, you are seeing me as I looked at that time.

Together with a number of kindred spirits—men and women of various ages and backgrounds—I had formed the Paine Society *some years earlier. What we all had in common was a passion for freedom coupled with deep dismay with the prevalence of physical coercion in our respective lands and, indeed, in the world at large. A number of us were enormously wealthy as a result of lifetimes giving rein to fiercely entrepreneurial spirits.*

In forming this society, we adopted as our rallying cry the immortal words of American patriot, Thomas Paine. We have it in our power to begin the world over again, Paine had proclaimed. And we took the last six words as our formal charter: To begin the world over again.

All of us welcome you to hear, see, and understand our story. This is our legacy. We want you to understand the necessary and sufficient conditions we had to provide in order to make this grand endeavor happen. Perhaps you will become a part of it. This is the story of The Prometheus Frontier and its beginning—

The image went to tiny dots, before evaporating into the air. Alek found that he was alone. Sunbeams were now finding their way into the garden through the thick foliage of its side borders. There was a soft profusion of sound from birds and insects. From the far end, he heard waves gently heaving against the cliffs below his line of sight. The garden gathered the sound and amplified it. Alek thought of auditory waves emanating from that other island, calling for attention across ten miles of salt air.

The next portal plate read *Marek*. As he entered the program, looping images passed before Alek's eyes from different angles. A narrative voice began, and the moving stills became a vidstream of his great-grandfather in different settings over the years. Other voices entered as well, all of them animated, but gently so—with a hushed, intimate quality.

Marek Rankl had been the archetype of the man of thought in action. He had produced an immense fortune, animated by the joy of productive work, of the *action*—the exhilaration of using his mind, creating new technologies and new processes and new industries. And now he was creating the ultimate: a new nation. He was a man of enormous energy and infectious vitality.

He was also a complex man. Single-mindedly serious in his work and convictions, he was nonetheless ready to burst into laughter at any moment. A colleague once said that if you ever heard Marek Rankl's laughter, you never forgot it. Alek heard sudden laughter in the background and smiled. He knew, from the richness of the timbre of it, that here was his great-grandfather probably more than a century ago.

In his rare leisure moments, Rankl took an almost childlike pleasure in having fun and in trying new things. He loved to give pleasure and found the look on a woman's face during the ultimate moments, and indeed the radiance of her entire body, the most beautiful sight in nature. Alek smiled when he heard these last words spoken by a soft woman's voice.

Then a more energetic voice came in. Marek Rankl was the man the poet had in mind whom people "wish long and long to be with," whom they yearn to sit by in the boat that he and they might touch. A friend once compared him to Aristotle's great-souled man. Another compared him to the man responding to Cyrano's cry, "Bring me Giants!"—not because of the size of Marek's body, which was sharply defined but average—rather it was because he was a man in love with life on a grand scale.

The narrative voices and accompanying vidstreams then segued to his early years. A slightly out-of-breath girl's voice explained that, as a child, Marek Rankl was consumed by everything scientific. He read widely on his own and his parents, who were academics, delighted in stoking his endless curiosity.

He was astonished to discover that the ancient Earth went through a long period during which its crust was totally under water and that the mean depth of this water was two miles. And he was further intrigued to learn that now, billions of years later, nearly three quarters of planet Earth was *still* under water of the same mean depth.

A boy's voice was next to pick up the narrative. Marek's young mind, it explained, was ever questioning, ever drilling more deeply. He wondered what the origin of all this water was, before realizing there was an earlier question: What was the origin of planet Earth. This took him to the theory of stellar evolution. He learned that Earth, its oceans, and all living things, were once the stuff of stars, broadcast as dust into intergalactic space by supernovas—dying stars exploding in their final bursts of glory.

When he learned that two of the most common elements in this dust were the highly reactive elements, hydrogen and oxygen—hydrogen the *most* common—he suddenly realized where the vast oceans, which after all were composed of these two elements, must have come from. His father, himself a scientist, marveled at his son's insight.

The girl's voice came back in, to relate that Marek next asked himself: Out of all this water, where did land come from? And now he was taken to the science of Geology. Tectonic plates drove the evolution of mountains and deep ocean trenches and continents. Finally, it was inevitable that he would wonder where life came from. And for this answer, he found he had to go back to the oceans—*ever* the oceans, he realized.

He learned that life's complex biochemistry originated out of simpler chemical reactions in the ancient ocean, reactions triggered by titanic electric bolts in the primordial atmosphere—*lightning*. These led to self-replicating molecules and eventually simple cells. All this took place relatively early in the history of the planet.

The two young voices continued to alternate in their conveying of the young Marek's story. It was no surprise to Marek's parents that microbiology became an overarching passion for their young son. The ubiquitous microbe fascinated him. He discovered that microbes—microscopic living organisms—exist in every part of the biosphere. And he was intrigued to learn that the more primitive of them, those without nuclei, still accounted for more than a quarter of the entire biomass on present-day Earth.

Virology, a vast subspecialty of microbiology, consumed Marek's imagination next. He learned that viruses, though not independent living organisms, were nonetheless the main driver of genetic diversity—of evolution—through their ability to transfer genes between organisms. Viruses were known to be ancient, having originated before the divergence of life into the two great domains of nucleated and non-nucleated organisms. This especially captured the imagination of the young Marek.

Viruses, he learned did not replicate apart from living matter and, conversely, most living matter did not evolve without the driving power of viruses. "Father, did you know that more than half the human genome—perhaps as much as seventy-five percent—is known to come from ancient viral invasions," the preteen Marek expounded, "and that a teaspoon of seawater alone contains ten million viruses!" Alek, wearing his virtual headset, heard the different voice of a young boy and immediately identified with his excitement. He knew it was the voice of Marek at that age.

―――

A somewhat authoritative woman's voice was next to pick up the narrative. Marek Rankl was seven years old, it pointed out, when his mother, a Classical Greek scholar, deemed it time to introduce her son to Aristotle's scientific works—Aristotle: the first serious biologist. Somehow, she was not surprised to find that he was especially intrigued by the philosopher's *De Anima*, his biological treatise on human animation or *soul*. Aristotle, he learned, regarded *soul* as an entirely natural phenomenon, *not* supernatural. Philosophy became another passion for the young Marek, a passion that he was never to sate fully.

And now it was a man's deep voice relating that, shortly after Aristotle, another philosopher consumed Marek, this time introduced by his father. She had been a great champion of reason and freedom in the previous century. It was from this thinker that he first heard the concept of *good* defined—that whatever promoted human life, was good and that whatever diminished it, was evil. He was too young to see that this was the product of great inductive generalizations. For him it was simply self-evident.

———

Alek Rankl, standing before his great-grandfather's holo-lasic portal, suddenly felt the need to break, and he allowed his attention to switch back to the present. The program seemed to perceive the change in his focus and, as if sensing its cause, a quiet voice said, Yes, this has been a flood of information. But, as you'll see, it's all vital if you're to understand Marek Rankl, the man. This presentation especially dwelt on his pursuit of philosophy and marine microbiology because these sciences are so foundational to the arc of his life. The coming portals will make that clear.

And with that, Alek returned to the sights, scents, and sounds of Oribel Island.

———

MAREK

Breakfast that first morning on Oribel was at the kitchen end of a long open room. It ran the full length of the cliff dwelling.

Wood predominated throughout—walls, flooring, furniture, even the ceiling. The warm honey shades on all surfaces created an overall feeling of intimacy, despite the expansiveness of the room.

A line of louvered windows, interrupted by two glass balcony doors, also louvered, ran from the kitchen to the far end. The open louvers faced north to the Caribbean and invited salt air into the room. Arête was a pale blue strip on the horizon.

The long wall opposite the windows had a hallway behind it leading to bedrooms, utility rooms, and reading rooms. An opening, midway in the hall, led to stairs and the lift.

Alek's arrival last night had been late, and breakfast was the first time he saw his aunt and uncle together. "Call me *Rhee*," she had told him, as she quickly engaged her nephew, her face animated with curiosity. There was a musical lilt to her voice, and her dark eyes were those of the Caribbean native, further deepened by their contrast with a startling mass of silver hair. Her feet were bare, and bright colors attired her small compact body. Her only jewelry was a blue topaz bracelet, and a gauzy wrap was around her otherwise bare shoulders. Her delivery of coffee to him, earlier, was too brief for him to notice, but now, really seeing her for the first time, Alek found himself drawn to her relaxed and subtly exotic style.

After eating, they lingered at the table. Alek's eyes took in the length of the room. His uncle pointed out, "Your great-grandfather and Jorge Besosa had their first meeting there many years ago. We affectionately call all this the *Long Room*. Marek's yacht captain, Armando Rojas, was present as well and did the watercolor you see on the rear wall, opposite the windows. It was one of his many talents."

Alek approached the painting and saw two men, drinks in hand, their faces illuminated by the light from the windows. Rojas had deftly captured the essence of Marek and the dark intensity of Besosa and, behind them, the Caribbean.

Returning to the breakfast table, Alek looked closely at his uncle and thought of the Marek he had seen in the portals. Eric was taller and quite lean, his skin tanned and leathery. But to Alek's eyes there was no mistaking the similarities. "You have Marek Rankl's mouth and eyes, Uncle. Also, you have his thick hair."

Alek glanced at Rhee's head and Eric, noticing, said, "No, your aunt's silver hair doesn't necessarily mean she's older than I. But isn't it a magnificent halo to go with her lovely face?" Alek saw their smiling eyes meet momentarily, the bond between them clear.

"Marek and Lenore originated the concept of a garden of windows, or portals," Rhee said. "You'll meet her in a later portal presentation, probably tomorrow. She and Marek, like all members of the Paine Society, were passionate about history. Ventana, which is a memorial garden of sorts, is their way of assuring that the saga of Arête's evolution never gets lost."

"They put a twist on the saying that those who cannot remember the past are condemned to repeat it," Eric pointed out. "Their twist was on the positive side of that old adage. For them: Only those who remember the past are able to sustain—and repeat—its successes."

"With emphasis on the *only*," Rhee added.

After breakfast, Eric and Alek went down the lift, to stroll the island. They passed the air vehicle pad and walked down to the pier where Marek Rankl's yacht, Oribel, had landed so many years ago. They turned and gazed back at the mountain from which they had just come. Eric explained the island's geology and the challenges of constructing the cliff dwelling and now, maintaining it. A sudden sound of spraying water caught their attention.

Not far offshore, two gigantic creatures rose from the ocean and twisted in the air before crashing back in. They repeated this and then repeated it again. "Breaching humpbacks," Eric said. "They mate here every year."

"I can see that" Alek replied, fascinated by the male's grand display of gigantic readiness—a wonder of nature, he thought to himself.

It was not until afternoon that Alek returned to Ventana Garden and the virtual world of its portals. The next plate read Ocean, and when he initiated it, Alek saw a stream of still photos, alternating with vid footage, of a large factory-like building in a congested city area.

As he was taken through the main entrance, a narrative voice introduced him to Ocean Polytechnic Institute of Brooklyn, whose main building had been a razor blade factory in the previous century.

But Marek Rankl did not select Ocean for the beauty of its campus. Indeed, it did not have one. Rather, he chose it for its renowned programs in marine science and research facilities. And he knew from the depth of his *own* research, on the Polytechnic itself, that the institute shared his conviction that the ubiquitous role of microbial life—for understanding, exploiting, and preserving Earth's vast oceans—was yet to be plumbed by the scientific world.

But there was another striking feature of Ocean Polytechnic. Of all the science institutions Marek reviewed, Ocean's humanities department especially stood out. He examined the course offerings, then their descriptions, then the credentials of the teachers, including professional output in their given fields.

He also noted the professors who were multi-disciplinary. This systematic evaluation revealed that the humanities department at Ocean Polytechnic was unparalleled. On all counts, Ocean was the logical choice.

Microbiology was not Marek Rankl's only passion. During his first two years, he also took a number of philosophy courses, first as electives, then for the sheer pleasure of it. He had discovered an inspiring philosophy professor who himself found inspiration in the twentieth century thinker Marek had discovered as a boy, through his father.

The professor was also a scholar of Ancient Greek philosophy. Until then, Marek's main exposure to the ancients had been Aristotle and Plato. Now, for the first time, he explored the pre-Socratics of that vibrant age.

Jumping forward in time, Marek also explored the Western Enlightenment and the Industrial Revolution to which it led. This exposed him to the broad literature of free enterprise, as the economic approach supremely suited for unleashing human potential. For the first time, Marek fully understood what had led his parents to emigrate from Poland.

Although marine microbiology was not Rankl's only passion, it was his greatest. Indeed, it continued to grow during his years at the Polytechnic. His master's thesis, *Microbial Driven Symbiotic Mutualism of Blue Fin Tuna and Marine Kelp in Farm Environments*, was a product of that passion. Much work had already been done in the fields of fish and algae farming. What was new in Marek Rankl's work was their integration, using microbial action to drive a unique and unprecedented symbiosis.

The department head urged Marek to develop it further in Ocean's doctoral program. But Marek Rankl had other ideas. He had already caught the eyes of venture capitalists. Alek heard the narrative voice replaced with his great-grandfather's actual voice.

Ventana

Thank you, Professor, but I'm starting my own company, and further research will be in my own labs, with my own scientists. It was not long after he received his Master of Science in Marine Microbiology that Marek Rankl launched Rankle Marine Enterprises.

The next portal plate simply read *RME*. After its founding, Rankl Marine Enterprises grew exponentially, year by year.

Alek became completely immersed in its story and its people. Marek Rankl was famous for his creative genius and boundless energy. But other qualities soon became evident as well. There was his conviction that every achievement was, at root, the result of the focused *individual* mind. Rankl Marine Enterprises never failed to stress individual effort. It strongly encouraged team effort as well—with the dynamic interactions a team approach made possible—but the fundamental role of the individual was never forgotten. It was never viewed as inconsequential, simply because it was individual.

Marek Rankl rejected the prevailing notion that human nature was inherently weak and depraved. He built honesty and integrity into his company's code of ethics, as fundamental virtues never to be compromised. RME recruiters were skilled in probing for those qualities. And conversely, the reputation of Rankl Marine Enterprises invited men and women who lived by those virtues to seek out RME.

By his mid-forties, Marek Rankl was a billionaire many times over, and his company one of the richest in the world. As one journalist put it, Marek Rankl got his start with key infusions of venture capital, and finally, he himself, became the Venture Capitalist of all venture capitalists.

Across the decades, Rankl the corporation evolved into three major enterprises. Its Fish Aquaculture Division developed the first fully successful microbial-driven processes for safely and hygienically cultivating and raising giant blue fin tuna. Its scientists then tailored those processes to do the same with many other species, each of which had its own unique challenges. Many of them had been overfished across the years. Rarely, were such challenges not overcome, and testing invariably indicated that Rankl Marine Enterprises was the gold standard in the world of fish aquaculture.

Rankl's second major enterprise was its Marine Agronomy Division. The farming of seaweeds and other algae for food—human and animal—and as a source of bio-fuel—had been in existence for centuries. Rankl scientists revolutionized this industry as well.

RME's New Venture Division was its third major enterprise. Over the years there was a steady flow of new ventures out of its science laboratories and test facilities. There had been the problem of waste in the world's oceans, from empty plastic containers. RME scientists designed an inexpensive process which embedded a dormant and harmless form of plastic-eating bacteria in the plastic used for containers. The bacteria did not become active until the plastic hit ocean water, from which point it quickly disappeared, with no harmful byproduct of its own.

There had been the tragedy of long-term reef loss in the world's oceans. RME designed diagnostic tools to determine cause—pathogenic or environmental—and treatment kits for completely restoring the reef over time. Both diagnosis and treatment involved the use of microbial-based tools. So successful were the prototype projects that reef reclamation had become a new industry. Never were the reefs of the world more flourishing.

The list went on. The innovative genius of Rankl scientists seemed inexhaustible. There had been seemingly insurmountable problems with the technology of floating islands. Many of these problems had to do with waste management. For these, RME scientists drew on their array of innovations in fish aquaculture and marine agronomy. For every process there was an unavoidable waste product that needed management. RME, with its vast knowledge banks, was supremely positioned to revolutionize waste management as well.

It became a common perception that RME scientists and engineers, could directly, economically, and successfully solve most challenges.

The portal presentation had ended, and Alek Rankl found himself on Oribel again. He knew he needed to stop for the day, to digest all that he had learned. But first, he decided to read the remaining portal plates, to get a fix on what was ahead. When he finished, he found that the plates had taken him to the far end of the garden where he could see Arête as a golden glow on the late afternoon horizon.

Then to his left, he saw an opening in the foliage, to a meadow which was alive with dappled sunlight. A short distance in, he saw two human figures, and when he approached them, he saw a bronze sculpture. Two life-sized nudes, male and female, stood two feet apart. Each body leaned toward the other, as they held up their wine glass to touch above their heads in a salute. The touching wine glasses established the only point of contact—but for their eyes.

The figures were mature but so exquisitely rendered that they could have been in the full bloom of youth. Alek recognized Marek and knew the woman must be Lenore. He had seen her name a few minutes ago, on the next portal plate.

Slowly, he circled the sculpture and stopped at a black granite bench. The figures stood on a slab of the same stone. And cut into its polished edge, was the salute for which their clinking glasses was the exclamation point.

To a life, which is a reason unto itself.

It was followed by two small letters, barely discernable: *AR*. He sat on the stone bench, stunned by the nine words. He turned them over in his mind and, for long minutes, considered their implications. Everything else around him had faded away.

LENORE

As he walked from Ventana garden to the lift, Alek Rankl's mind was still on the sculpture. How often I have pondered the meaning of life only to have it laid to rest by those nine simple words, he asked himself.

He fell face down on his bed. It had been a long day. As he started to doze off, he heard an air vehicle landing, as if delivering a message. His last thought was the salute: *To a life ...*

He found Eric alone in the long room, the setting sun slanting in from the west. "Rhee will join us in a bit," his uncle informed him. "She has a visitor from Arête, and they're down in the Neuron Center. They'll join us shortly." He saw the question forming on Alek's mouth and added, "You'll see Neuron later this week."

"I found the sculpture of Marek and Lenore," Alek told his uncle.

"That's another work of Armando Rojas," his uncle pointed out. "He painted, he sculpted, and he was a landscape designer. He designed interiors as well. Ventana Garden is his design, as is the interior of Marek's duplex apartment in New York City. Tomorrow's portal is going to take you there."

"It looks like Armando is also an artist with words," Alek said. "I saw his initials on the sculpture's base, after the words of the salute." His uncle shook his head. "Ah, but Armando never signs or initialed his work. Whether he was being modest, or whether he thought his work so distinct that he didn't *have* to sign it—I suspect it was the latter—but I'm not sure. What I *do* know is that the initials are not his. The sculpture is, but not the salute. He got that from somewhere else."

They were interrupted as Rhee came into the room with a much younger woman, introducing her with, "Joan Liang, meet Alek Rankl." Alek saw a serious face. "You're meeting your first native born Arêtean, Nephew," Eric informed him, "except for your Aunt Rhee. And Joan goes by her surname. She likes to be called Liang."

"And I'm meeting my first Rankl who is not an Arêtean," Liang said, as she took his hand. When they touched, her serious look suddenly lit with an impossibly radiant animation, the way some faces do, when they break into a smile.

She wore brief shorts and a cotton top that left one shoulder bare. Mere sandals protected her feet, but her well-defined thighs and the way she held herself seemed to poise her entire body for action, at any moment. Alek noticed there was a taut power to her. Then she excused herself, and said to Rhee, "I'll get back to you as soon as we understand the problem better."

The evening meal was food that Liang had brought from Aréte. Her original plan, to join them, had been changed. As she lifted off in her air vehicle, she hovered off the balcony and waved its wings before turning for Aréte. Alek's eyes followed. He watched her become an ever-smaller speck above Aréte, until finally she became one with it.

After eating, they went out onto the balcony. Stars filled a moonless sky. Every few minutes, Alek's eyes returned to the

Lenore

brighter sky over Arête City, ten miles away. A single light, slightly closer, caught his eye, then caught it again. Suddenly he realized it was the flame.

He slept well that night and was back in Ventana a half hour before sunrise at the next portal, *Marek & Lenore.*

Ocean Polytechnic's cafeteria had its usual midday congestion. Alek's virtual headset filled his ears with the sounds of clinking plates and buzzing conversation. A table had just become empty, and two diners headed for it, food trays in hand. They nearly collided. The woman immediately recognized Marek Rankl and was stunned to be meeting him like this.

Quickly recovering, she said, "Table mates?"

He bowed and pulled a chair away from the table with a flourish and a *"Mademoiselle,"* as he held it for her.

"Why, thank you, Sir," she said, in response to his mock gallantry.

She informed him that her name was Lenore Pellon and that she was the philosophy professor in the Polytechnic's humanities department. A few probing questions and he was able to confirm her intellectual orientation. And she, his, simply from the nature of his questions. He explained that he was at Ocean Poly with one of his colleagues, seeking to lure future graduates to Rankl Marine Enterprises.

"It's not every day that I have lunch with the most famous Polytechnic graduate," she told him.

"*Infamous* is more the concept usually pinned on me, Professor."

"Not by me."

"Thank you, but I am afraid you are in the minority, certainly among intellectuals at least. Most of them are convinced that humans need the strong hand of outside authority to guide and control them. I am *not* of that persuasion."

"You know philosophy, Mr Rankl. I could tell that from your interrogation of me. Where does that come from?"

"Please, call me Marek. To answer your question, it started quite early, from my mother. Her field was Classical Greece. When I was seven, she actually introduced me to Aristotle's *De Anima*. She wanted to augment the quest for scientific knowledge I had already been on, from when I was even younger—not long after I started to walk, in fact. Aristotle's treatise on the soul fascinated me. That was when I first saw a great philosopher in action. And my father, even though his field was Physics, introduced me to others. Now, so many years later, love of philosophy is in my genes."

Then he added, "You know, Professor Lenore Pellon, I see you following in a sort of tradition at Ocean Polytechnic. In my college days here, two decades ago, the lone philosophy professor was also of your intellectual bent. I took all his courses and ended up with a second major, in philosophy. Intellectually, it was a most exciting time for me."

"I teach a night course on Aristotle," she said. "Why don't you sit in this evening?"

"I might be a bit late," he replied, "but I will be there."

Lenore

With mock gravity she assured him, "Fear not. Being tardy won't affect your grade."

Professor Lenore Pellon was a woman on the verge of forty whose greatest passion was the history of ideas. Alek felt the augmented pull of the portal drawing him into her life, with a steady vidstream of images, a combination of still and moving. In her career she found herself very much the outsider, a female narrative voice informed him. This became especially evident when she published her first book, based on her PhD dissertation.

The book was titled *Post-Post Modernism and the Advancing Decline of the West*. Her theme was that this decline was due to the West's abandonment of the Enlightenment's reverence for human reason, followed by an almost gleeful pleasure in the ever-accelerating nihilism that resulted.

In person, Pellon's voice was strong and offset a diminutive height. It was also slightly musical, in the way of the island cultures of the Caribbean, from which her parents had come. She moved with a grace earned by years of gymnastics and athletics. She excelled in any physical activity by daring, fleetness of foot, and the extraordinary levitating power of her jumps. This last offset her modest height and served her and her college's basketball program especially well. As she matured, exuberant vitality remained an integral part of her style as a person. So too did the somewhat wild dark hair, kept on the short side by her own hand.

As a young adult, Lenore Pellon reveled in physical challenges and the mental preparation needed to mitigate risks, whatever they were. She enjoyed rock climbing, for the physical and mental discipline required.

Lenore

She flirted with wingsuit BASE jumping, for the sheer exhilaration of soaring off a mountain, her outstretched body gliding downward, possessed by the gravity to which she had surrendered herself, until deploying her parachute at the last moment. But she soon abandoned this sport, realizing that ever-improving wingsuit designs and training still left too many risks.

She turned to spelunking—cave exploration—to conquer the fear of confined spaces, seeing it as the exact opposite of jumping *off* mountains—going *into* them instead. In one of these caves, in the Pyrenees, she flung herself headlong into the rushing water and black terror of a subterranean river until disgorged into brilliant sunlight, a short distance down the mountain's face.

On the wall behind her desk at Ocean, pictures captured such escapades, and Alek's virtual headset took him fully into them. He experienced the movement, the fear, the thrill, the cold. Suddenly, he was flying in the air himself and looking down on Marek Rankl and Lenore Pellon. Marek was in a wingsuit this time, with his arms and legs outstretched. And she was astride his back, riding her stallion, with shorts, T-shirt, helmet, and parachute pack the only garb on her body. Then she hurled her head back and pointed her face upward into the sun as Marek, and now Alek, more than seventy-five years later, heard her long cry of ecstasy.

Lenore

The narrative voice concluded then, indicating to Alek that he had witnessed Marek's only flirtation with this thrilling, but dangerous sport. He had also witnessed Lenore's last ride. Alek smiled, and after a pause, a male voice continued the narrative.

There was something in Professor Lenore Pellon's Aristotle class that long-ago evening that Marek Rankl, even many years later, would take pleasure in recounting. She had just taught Aristotle's famous argument of reaffirmation through denial when a slouched student lazily raised his hand and said, "What if I simply choose *not* to accept Aristotle's law of contradiction, that nothing can be A and non-A at the same time and in the same respect? What if I don't have a problem with contradictions?"

Lenore

Marek saw the curled upper lip and supercilious attitude of the college student who was above such a triviality as logic. But Pellon simply looked at him and answered, "Then you'll have no difficulty when I test your understanding of that law, and of Aristotle's case that any denial of it merely *reaffirms* it. You'll have no problem seeing the *F* grade on your test booklet as an A."

The incident was etched in Marek Rankl's mind, never to be forgotten. It had to do with a short-haired, captivating woman, Lenore Pellon, professor of philosophy at Ocean Polytechnic Institute, on the edge of a new phase in her life, though she did not know it at that moment.

It had to do with her absolute self-possession, a command of whatever she was doing, and an ability to think on her feet that was second nature. It was as second nature as the fluidity of her body whenever she moved. Marek Rankl knew, at that moment, with the laser certainty of the self-evident, that he would have this woman in his life—for the rest of his life.

VINDAUGE

When Alek Rankl initiated the next portal, *Vindauge*, a hololasic visual field embraced him once again. He was in an air vehicle, and the only sound was the low hum of its hydrogen engines.

He was several hundred feet above the ocean, steadily approaching New York City from a southerly direction. The skyline in the near distance grew larger as the AV passed over the Verrazzano bridge and then a bit later the Statue of Liberty. Finally, the AV started up the Hudson. Alek saw the traffic below, on the roadway running parallel to the river.

Shortly above midtown, they banked to starboard, flying east for two avenues, and paused in hover mode near the top level of an eighty-story glass tower. A soft and resonant male voice pointed out that on this particular morning, a middle-aged Marek Rankl was in the tower's duplex penthouse. This was his New York residence, and from the time of its conception, he had called the tower *Vindauge*. It was the international headquarters of Rankl Marine Enterprises and the primary residence of a number of RME executives and scientists as well.

The portal took Alek into a study where he found Marek Rankl sitting before a large, wall-mounted screen. His eyes, however, were on the panoramic outside view. He was looking to the George Washington Bridge in the near distance, gleaming in the sun, as commuter traffic streamed into the city. Bringing his eyes back to the screen, he called for a slow, audio scroll. He listened to the flow of the words, stopping it occasionally for a final tweak, using a keypad.

Then Marek Rankl sat motionless. He was lost in his thoughts, and Alek heard his great-grandfather's inner voice. My whole life, the voice began, has been a preparation for this—the most important piece of writing I have ever done. This is my declaration of defiance to the world. No single business setback has brought me to this point. Rather it has been an accumulation of egregious coercive acts. The evil of initiated physical coercion by man against man must be stopped, and this Declaration is the essential first step. This Declaration is the philosophy. This Declaration of freedom—one thousand words—is the starting point and cornerstone of my vision to begin the world over again. Without these one thousand words it would be doomed to failure. Hell, without them, the vision would not even get off the ground.

There was a long pause before Marek's inner voice resumed. *To begin the world over again*—I remember so vividly when I first saw those words—my student days at Ocean Polytechnic. I remember the leisure reading I did to refresh myself during those years. Philosophy and its application to world affairs was so much of it. My second passion after microbiology was always philosophy.

And I remember the first time I saw those words. I had been immersed in Thomas Paine's *Common Sense* when they hit me—*We have it in our power to begin the world over again*—the most optimistic words I had ever heard. And I feel the same way today, these many years later—just as strongly—if anything, I feel them even *more* strongly.

At that point, the portal's narrative voice resumed. After completing his studies at Ocean, all Marek's energy went into Rankl Marine Enterprises. RME: his business world, the world of industry, of new processes, of new systems. It was a wildly exciting, unlimited world which totally consumed him, as he continually expanded.

And so, Marek effectively forgot those twelve words. But they were not lost. They were twelve seeds planted in his subconscious, waiting to germinate—later—when the time was right.

We have it in our power to begin the world over again.

A firm but soft female voice picked up the narrative, and Alek listened closely. He also watched closely, enjoying the visual augmentation, as it moved between video stills and footage of locations, objects, and events—all deftly synced with the narrative voice.

After their initial meeting at Ocean Polytechnic, Marek Rankl and Lenore Pellon regularly made time in their schedules to meet. They would rendezvous at a restaurant in the city, away from Vindauge. He had a private table where they could talk with few distractions. They explored each other's mind and values and work. They explored what each held dear, an activity often occupying them for hours—favorite fiction, music, foods—favorite poems, historians, philosophers.

But work was the subject to which they most often returned. They talked about the pervasive regulatory repression throughout the world of business and finance and how it affected productive enterprises. They talked about the ever-intensifying attempts by government and private entities to pirate intellectual property. They talked about the endemic environmental activism and anti-trust suits, both of which mired industry in endless court battles. *His* work environment.

Vindauge

They talked about the ever-declining intellectual capability of students and intellectuals in general and how this affected the academic world. They talked about her great passion, the history of ideas, and that no matter where you look, you find historical revisions, outright falsehoods, and the ignorance they spawn. *Her* work environment.

She looked at him and knew his experience was the same. Still, she felt compelled to add, "I'm telling you, Marek Rankl, in my darkest moments, I sometimes think that Western civilization is in a death spiral, so advanced that it is virtually irreversible." Alek saw Marek's head nodding, as the female narrative voice continued.

Early in their dinners together, Marek Rankl saw that Dr Lenore Pellon was the logical recipient for his Declaration of Freedom. But he waited until she was between semesters before sending it. The e-com to which he attached it explained that it was not just a declaration of defiance but above all, the setting forth of a vision. "I need you to critique this with your professional philosopher's hat on," he wrote. "Including the vision it advances."

Lenore was intrigued. But recalling their dinners, and the occasional allusions to something he had been writing for years, she was not surprised. Immediately, she opened the attachment and began to read. The vidstream faded out.

After a long pause, a new stream slowly faded in, but without narrative voice. Alek found he was a passenger in the rear of a sedan. He had a view through the windshield, between Armando Rojas who is driving and Lenore Pellon. The New York skyline was in the near distance, straight ahead.

Vindauge

They were approaching the dark maw of the tunnel under the East River from Brooklyn, where Lenore lived, to Manhattan. Then suddenly, two minutes later, the vehicle burst into blinding light on the other side of the river. Alek imagined Lenore reliving her subterranean river dive in the Pyrenees, which also ended by exploding into sunlight.

The female narrative voice resumed briefly, to explain the purpose of their journey, and then went silent. Lenore had given feedback to Marek on his declaration. She would neither delete nor reword any of it. It was a model of precision and clarity. But she had suggested additions, and they would discuss them this evening, in Vindauge. It would be Lenore's first visit to the tower, a building which had long fascinated her.

As the vehicle headed north, Alek could see Vindauge in the distance and beyond it, the George Washington Bridge. He could see that each of Vindauge's eighty floors was a square, no bigger or smaller than any of the others. Yet, viewed as a whole, the overall structure seemed to be spiraling up out of the city's bedrock.

Curious, Alek looked more closely as they gradually approached it. Finally, he saw that each floor was offset ten feet from the structure's center of gravity, in a direction that, every five floors changed by ninety degrees. He could see that it was this which produced the spiraling illusion—especially when viewing the structure from an angle—an experience afforded a number of times by the slightly winding roadway on which they were traveling.

Alek, from his rear seat, could see Lenore's amused profile as she watched the tower's changing appearance. He saw it too and smiled. The structure conveyed a palpable sense of twisting motion. There was a sense of play about it.

Vindauge

He heard an exchange of words between Lenore and Armando. She knew it was safe to assume Marek lived at the top of Vindauge, but other than that, she had no idea what to expect. Armando glanced at her but remained noncommittal. "He wants you to explore his home for yourself," he told her.

From the garage, Alek found himself in a private elevator with Armando and Lenore. Armando exited to his apartment near the top of the tower; Lenore continued up to Marek's entry gallery on the seventy-ninth floor.

From the entry gallery, Lenore looked down the hall to her right and could hear activity in the kitchen. She knew Marek was plying one of his favorite leisure activities. When she reached the kitchen door, however, she saw a small sign that was built into it. It read, *Por favor, do not disturb*, in colorful letters. Underneath, clearly for her benefit, there was a handwritten note: *All tours are self-guided.*

Lenore returned the way she had come and made her way into the Great Room. It was the shape of a large, inverted letter L, the short base of which was a dining area facing the Hudson River. The other side of the river was the state of New Jersey and the start of the American continent. The George Washington Bridge was a short distance upriver.

The long leg of the L extended east to west and faced south. Lenore took in the view. In the distance, she saw Pangaia Island, near the tip of Manhattan. And on the far horizon, the graceful arc of the Verrazzano Bridge connected Brooklyn and Staten Island. The Atlantic Ocean lay beyond.

All exterior walls of the tower consisted of six-foot-wide, floor-to-ceiling sheets of a crystal-clear material. The narrow separations between sheets were barely visible and thus, from any direction, the tower presented the outside world panoramically. *Vindauge*, Alek heard Lenore's inner voice

Vindauge

recalling, is derived from the Old Norse word for *wind's eye*, eventually to become *window*. How perfect, she said to herself, as the view held her captive.

Throughout the tower, voice controls enabled the production of a gentle shade when desired. All rooms on this level had been subdued to a mellow glow, and Lenore had the feeling she was in the living area of a Caribbean villa in midafternoon.

All decorating touches were by someone who had a special feeling for that part of the world. Alek who now, more than three quarters of a century later, had virtually joined Lenore on her self-guided tour, knew from what his uncle had told him that it is Armando Rojas. His were the floral designs on cushions, the wall colors, and those of the thick rugs. But almost everything was understated, muted. The colors tended toward pastels. Dramatic tones were limited to accents and were sparsely scattered, as if at random, on a wall here, or an end table there, or on a corner of carpet.

Two large aquariums displayed the seemingly impossible colors of exotic marine life. One of them came up out of the floor and provided support for a sizeable coffee table; the other, twelve feet long, was built into an interior wall of the great room.

Furniture was oversized, and chairs were adjustable in subtle ways to enable optimal comfort. Lamps were few and simple. A Chopin Nocturne played somewhere in the background. The overall ambiance was one of calm.

Lenore Pellon, Alek realized, already had a fair fix on the man she knew as Marek Rankl. This was the rest of the story. There was a heightened intimacy by virtue of his leaving it up to her to explore at will. She found that all doors, other than the kitchen, were ajar. She was a tourist, openly invited by the owner to explore his living space—to explore *him*.

Vindauge

She went from bedrooms and bathrooms to studies and reading nooks. She stopped at bookshelves, built into walls. At one of them, she randomly pulled out an advanced text on virology. Alek looked over her shoulder as she read the inscription. The book was a gift from his parents on his ninth birthday. Thumbing through it, she expressed astonishment when she saw the detailed marginalia on various pages, in a boy's young hand. "But of course," Alek heard her voice say.

A glistening spiral staircase, metal-railed, reminded her she was in a duplex. It invited her upward. Near the top, the steps curved toward the adjacent wall, on which a vibrant watercolor hung. It caught her eye and riveted her in place. Two breeching whales, humpbacks, were mating, obviously in the throes of passion. There was no signature on the painting, but its brass plate read *New Beginnings.*

Alek was below her on the stairs, and seeing what made Lenore pause, he remembered the two whales he had seen off Oribel yesterday; he knew from the style of this work that he was seeing another Rojas watercolor.

When Lenore reached the upper floor, she walked into a spacious conference room. Its rear windows looked across the city toward the East River. The river itself was not visible, but the now-illuminated bridges to New York's outer boroughs *were.* Beyond them, Alek knew that Long Island reached more than one hundred miles east, into the Atlantic.

From the conference room, there were a number of bedrooms for overnight guests, each with its own bathroom. A large living room and media room were off a kitchen. Then, coming full circle, she was again at the spiral stairs.

Returning to the lower level, Lenore found her host standing, watching the setting sun. She saw that he had prepared a simple meal, now awaiting them in the dining area. Covered crockery

Vindauge

kept the product of his labor hot, and she detected the aroma of Caribbean spices.

A crystal decanter of red wine was on a side table. Marek Rankl turned to his guest with a smile. He poured and, as they held up their glasses to toast, the wine caught the sun and lit their faces with a warm glow.

The portal presentation ended. Alek Rankl realized that the scene he had just witnessed was a virtual re-enactment of Armando Rojas's sculpture in Ventana garden—so near to where he stood at this moment, nearly a century later—but for one thing.

Marek Rankl and Lenore Pellon had just toasted *To New Beginnings* ....

———

DECLARATION

The next portal took Alek Rankl into the dining area of his great-grandfather's Vindauge Tower penthouse. Marek Rankl and Lenore Pellon, their meal now finished, sat facing each other over coffee.

Again, there was no narrative voice. Alek knew he would be a first-hand witness to the drama that was about to begin.

Lenore reached for her attaché case. She opened it and removed two sets of paper. Each set had three sheets clipped together. She slid one across the table to Marek and laid the other on the table in front of herself. They unclipped the sheets and spread them out side by side, one sheet for each part of the Declaration: *Foundational Truths, The Case for a New Start*, and *Separations and Oath*.

She said, "As you requested, I highlighted my additions in order to make them stand out. But I didn't change a single word of your declaration. There was no need to do that."

"It is *our* Declaration now," he replied. "I looked carefully at your additions, as soon as you sent them, and I agree unreservedly with each of them. You now have the floor, Dr Pellon."

She sipped her coffee, collecting her thoughts. Then, "I want to start with a few general points. To begin, I like that, basically, you broke the document into three parts. Thomas Jefferson did the same with his iconic Declaration of Independence.

Declaration

I also like that you kept touches of his language, some of it legalistic and some of it simply verbal flourishes common in his day. I think that any reader or listener of our Declaration will recognize those nods to Jefferson's great achievement." He smiled at her use of *our*.

"But far more importantly, our Declaration would not be possible without the great intellectuals of the twentieth century—especially the one you and I have discussed so often.

"In Part One, you have lucidly preserved the fundamental concepts underpinning freedom," Lenore continued. I'm talking about the very meaning of *freedom* itself. Political freedom, correctly conceived, means freedom from initiated physical coercion. *Not* freedom from need. Freedom from need, as a political ideal, inevitably requires forcing someone to meet the needs of someone else. And that is a dreadful perversion of freedom. Freedom from need necessarily involves initiated coercion.

"I'm talking about the essential nature of rights. That a right morally sanctions *individual* action in a social context. Rights are not moral sanctions for some group, as a group, to demand an object or service that others must then provide.

That's a perversion of the very concept of *rights*. In a moral society, only individuals have rights. So-called group rights unavoidably violate individual rights—an evil always to be shunned.

"I'm talking about government limited to one fundamental function, namely, securing and protecting individual rights. That is, government separated from all other human endeavors.

"Clearly, Marek Rankl, you've captured the essential underlying concepts necessary for the birth and then the flourishing of the Prometheus Frontier."

Declaration

DECLARATION OF FREEDOM
PART ONE: FOUNDATIONAL TRUTHS

When in the course of human events, the nation that was once the freest the world has ever seen, whose government—a Constitutional Republic—was the first and only one in history explicitly founded on the moral principle of individual rights—when that nation, for centuries the sole beacon for the world's oppressed—when that nation itself loses sight of what it means to be free and, instead, makes initiated physical coercion and the violation of individual rights a way of life—it is then necessary to restart freedom in a new place.

We the men and women of the Prometheus Frontier hereby announce that we have given birth to such a place and proudly advance this Declaration of Freedom—freedom from initiated physical coercion—as its seminal founding document.

We hold certain fundamental truths to be observable and inducible facts of reality:

—that all individuals are born equal in their possession of reason, the distinguishing faculty elevating them above all other creatures,

—that individual human life—the ultimate value and standard of the good—in order to survive and to flourish, requires the free exercise of this faculty. For, unlike all other creatures, humans have no automatic knowledge of how to survive. Humans must use reason,

—that the initiation of physical coercion, because it abrogates the free exercise of reason and thereby human life, must be abolished from all human affairs as the ultimate evil,

—that standing in opposition to this evil are individual rights, which all men and women possess, the most fundamental of which are life, liberty, property, and the pursuit of happiness,

—that the absolute, objective basis of rights is not an alleged supreme being or social group or government but the immutable requirements for an individual human life to survive and flourish in a social context.

—that a constitutionally controlled government is an absolute necessity, strictly limited to the sole sacred purpose of securing and protecting individual rights against initiated physical coercion,

—that such a government equally protects all men and women against such coercion and itself uses force only in retaliation against those who have initiated that evil or have threatened to do so.

Declaration

"I had an idea you would say that," Marek said, "but it is good to hear you confirm it." He paused before adding, "Especially because it is from you." He thought he saw her eyes widen for an instant before she nodded her acknowledgment.

They discussed Lenore's additions, which were highlighted. Her first addition, in Part One, had to do with human life. "It is vital to include the fact that human life is the ultimate value and standard of good," she said. "It too is an observable and inducible foundational truth, along with the truths already identified, namely, that humans have no automatic knowledge of how to survive and must use reason to do so. Thus, do we make clear, why initiated physical coercion, the great enemy of reason—another induction—must be abolished from human affairs as the ultimate evil. Initiated physical coercion does not advance human life. Just the opposite, it diminishes and destroys it. And all too often, that death is a *slow* death.

Her second addition in Part One had to do with the objective basis of rights. "You already implicitly covered this issue in the previous paragraph," she pointed out. "But my additional words make it explicit that we rule out a supreme being, or government, or any other social group as the origin of rights.

In Part Two, they discussed Lenore's addition regarding property rights. And in Part Three, they discussed the statement of separations and the total prohibition of government involvement in the private sector. They discussed the sacred role of government to protect and retaliate against initiated physical force and what that entails.

They discussed the dangers to be faced by any country that makes bold to adopt this Declaration of Freedom. They discussed her passionate call to all people of good will throughout the world to join the *Prometheus Frontier* in its great quest.

Declaration

DECLARATION OF FREEDOM
PART TWO: THE CASE FOR A NEW START

When government itself makes it a practice to initiate physical coercion, or to legalize its initiation by others, it thereby becomes debased and must be replaced. We declare that throughout the world, governments exhibit this evil. Respect for reason demands that we set forth the evidence. To wit:

—Throughout the world, most nations pay lip service to rights in their constitutions, but then permit groups, even their own governments, to take them as sanctions to violate individual rights. This corrupts the meaning of rights which, when correctly understood, are only possessed by individuals. Correctly induced, rights protect the individual from the group, especially that largest and most powerful of groups—government.

—Property rights mean that individuals have the right to dispose of the product of their labor, or their earnings from it, as they see fit, providing they do not infringe or threaten the rights of others. Property rights protect individuals from slavery—slavery in any part of their lives, or in any portion. Property rights are moral sanctions for individuals to seek, gain, and dispose of the product of their work—not sanctions for some group to expropriate and dispose of it. Yet, throughout the world, throughout history, that evil is seen. Debased governments, and the groups they enable, regulate all sectors of their nation's life, including, in many nations, matters of religion or conscience. In developed nations, endemic public-private-sector cronyism produces corruption, coercive monopolies, and legalized plunder. Vast fiscal constituencies require countless government agencies and ever mounting debt. Cradle-to-grave dependence on government makes self-reliance—once a matter of cultural pride in more enlightened nations—a lost virtue. Pillaging from rampant pressure group warfare enervates entire cultures.

—The worldwide net effect of these depredations is incontrovertible: standards of living dramatically lower than what the wonders of modern science and technology make possible—standards of living compromised because the free exercise of reason through voluntary exchange has been preempted by initiated physical coercion.

Declaration

DECLARATION OF FREEDOM
PART THREE: SEPARATIONS AND OATH

We the founders of the Prometheus Frontier proudly proclaim this Declaration of Freedom and renounce initiated physical coercion. Indeed, our social system utterly outlaws it. Our social system enables all human interactions, with no exception, to take place through voluntary persuasion and trade by the free exercise of reason. That is, we proudly proclaim that Capitalism is, and always shall be, the social system of the Prometheus Frontier.

Our Constitution, for which this Declaration is the preamble, prohibits the government of the Prometheus Frontier from any function other than the defense of its nation states and their citizenry against any predatory force—whether from outside the Frontier or within. We accomplish this prohibition by constitutionally separating our government from finance, economy, education, medicine, science, religion, or any other activity or enterprise, including those yet to be developed.

We recognize that, as long as human nature is volitional, certain forces from within and without will initiate and threaten physical coercion. But our government exists to execute a sole sacred function. It addresses physical force initiated from within by a legal system of police and courts. It addresses physical force initiated from without by a lethal system of military defense. And the Prometheus Frontier will not want for impassioned citizens to defend freedom, with enlightened professionals leading the way on the intellectual and military ramparts.

As we set out on this grand endeavor, we the leaders of the Prometheus Frontier proudly adopt an exalted oath uttered long ago by the founders of the nation to which we alluded at the opening of this Declaration. It is fitting that we adopt their oath as our own, for the inspiration of their original founding is timeless.

We mutually pledge to each other our Lives, our Fortunes and our sacred Honor.

With these words ringing down through the ages, we know that all men and women of good will on Earth—East and West—will join us in our quest—our quest for a new Age of Reason—our quest to begin the world over again, with the birth of a new Enlightenment.

Declaration

Finally, Marek Rankl and Lenore Pellon sat in silence. He was the first to speak. "You know what we have done here, Lenore. We have preserved and advanced, in a mere one thousand words, philosophic principles that will drive the Prometheus Frontier in all the years before us."

He paused then, before continuing, "You know, of course, that I cannot imagine doing it without you. And that is because—you surely know this also—I cannot imagine *life* without you."

Their eyes locked, frozen for long moments. Finally, she spoke. "The first time we met at Ocean Polytechnic, that wasn't a chance meeting was it," she asked softly.

"No, my love, it was not."

The evening was a logical culmination and a new beginning. It was the logical culmination of a relationship which started in a college cafeteria several months earlier. It was a new beginning, high in a glass tower's master bedroom, of the rest of their life together.

It was a realization that had been growing and intensifying ever since they met. A mutual realization that they shared a soaring vision and the intense pleasure such a vision made possible. It was the intense pleasure of any striving for a supreme value—and more than that—of the exhilarating integration of mind and body, of *spirit* and body, required to achieve that value—and still more—of the indescribable joy of sharing it with a kindred spirit whose entire body, the vessel of that spirit, was convulsing with agonizing pulses of pleasure, impossible to exceed by the pleasure of any other human experience. Except that of witnessing it in the face, and body, of the spirit with whom it is being simultaneously shared.

NEURON

Eric and Rhee Rankl gazed over morning coffee through the sweeping windows of the long room.

The sun was bringing Arête into focus on the horizon. This was how they had started each day for the past three decades. Arête was, for them a great summation, an inextricable part of their lives, their shared history.

Besides being the home of Eric and Rhee during the past thirty years, Oribel was the site of a closely guarded secret facility. This facility was the nerve center of the Frontier's hard defense system. It was 175 feet below where they were now having breakfast.

Marek Rankl's first wife, Freda, had tragically died shortly after giving birth to twin sons, rather late in life. Each twin later fathered a son, one of whom was Erik, while the other was Alek's father.

After completing his education, in mathematics, Eric chose Arête as his home. Rhianna had been born on Arête. Her father was a native Arêtean, a well-known educator, while her mother had emigrated to Arête from Ethiopia. Both parents had inculcated in their daughter a love of learning, and so they were greatly pleased when her career choice was education.

Neuron

College and graduate school for Rhee had been overseas. But, like Eric Rankl, she loved Arête. Upon completing a doctorate in education, she returned to Arête. Her dissertation had been titled *The Science of Curriculum Development and Integration from Preschool through High School.*

Eric and Rhee had met through Angel and Livia Ramos. All four of them were kindred spirits, recognizing the fundamentality of education to everything else in human life. Each knew that education was the future of the island they loved.

Eric's doctorate was in Mathematics, and both he and Rhee lived and worked on Arête for twenty years, developing a system of floating islands just offshore the capital city's northern perimeter. These islands were floating schools and were in the shape of geodesic domes, and hence were referred to as *dome schools.*

They moved to Oribel thirty years ago to manage the Neuron Center administratively and liaise with the central defense functions in Arête City. Additionally, Eric was Neuron's resident mathematician, working closely with the Frontier's chief defense scientist. Rhee directed the Frontier's soft defense system from Oribel, with frequent trips each week to Arête.

Marek had originally given the *Neuron Center* its name. When Liang returned last night with the Frontier's lead defense scientist, they had gone to Neuron. Eric and Rhee saw them on their monitor now, still engrossed in the problem that had surfaced yesterday.

"It's time to introduce Alek to Neuron," Rhee said.

"I agree," her husband replied, as he left to go down to it. "Today's a perfect day, with our chief scientist on site. Why not bring him down after breakfast."

Neuron

When Alek arrived in the long room, he found that Rhee had prepared a plate for him. While he ate, they discussed yesterday's portals and the indispensable role of Lenore Pellon in the Frontier's history. "Lenore was, far and away, the best teacher I've ever had," Rhee told her nephew. "It was I who took the baton from her for the soft defense of Aréte, specifically the educational aspect of it in the Frontier. It has been my primary focus for the past three decades."

She noticed a questioning look and added, "By soft defense, I mean everything we do from a strictly intellectual standpoint to defend the Frontier. It contrasts with our hard defense system, the number one element of which, we know will fascinate you. In fact, it's why we waited so long to call you here." She saw that his quizzical look had only intensified and added, "You'll understand better by the end of the morning."

Rhee and Alek took the stairway down to Neuron. Unbeknownst to him, his aunt and uncle had been following him for years and knew more about him than he realized—a great deal more.

———

Alek had been born and raised in New York City, and his education, to age thirteen, had been at the Rankl Institute, just north of the city. Its curriculum, modeled on what Rhee Rankl had developed on Aréte decades earlier, drew students from all over the globe. Many were children of RME associates.

It was an expansive, mirror-like sliver of a building, dominated by windows of the same crystal-clear material as that of Vindauge Tower. Stretching parallel to the Hudson River, the structure was considerably longer than its height of seven stories. Its river side was devoted to classrooms and workshops. In each of them, the greatly elongated windows gave the students an unobstructed view of the Hudson. They also suggested that the institute's students had unobstructed access to another river, that of human knowledge.

The opposite side of the building, facing east, was dedicated to offices for teachers, administrators, and other functions. It also had the institute's main entrance, over which, there were ten chiseled words.

TO PREPARE THE CONCEPTUAL FACULTY FOR THE FULLY FLOURISHING LIFE

Education at the Rankl Institute spanned the years from early childhood to mid-teens. Alek began at age two. At the earliest ages, generously furnished workshops concentrated on the perceptual: motor skills at first, then basic life skills, then simple problem-solving skills.

The pace was unhurried and the ambiance peaceful. Teachers basically were guides. The children were free to work alone and to learn from their mistakes. They were allowed to take as much time as they needed, and interruption was kept to a minimum. Independence, self-sufficiency, and the ability to concentrate were the objectives. In addition, a growing sense of mental efficacy resulted, and this was the beginning of self-esteem.

Interaction, unforced, naturally occurred. Children discovered that they could learn from older children and they, in turn, could help the younger, with the pleasure and sense of efficacy that came with it.

As the children were learning to read, Phonics instruction was slowly introduced. This taught them the forty-four sounds—low level auditory concepts—or *phonemes*—of the English language. Phonemes enabled the sounding out of words without the guessing or memorization required by other approaches. Not long after, the foundational 3Rs of Reading, Writing, and Arithmetic were phased in.

By age five, students typically were ready to move into the Rankl Institute's core curriculum. Some students—Alek was one of them—were ready even earlier. The core areas were Mathematics, Science, Literature, and History. With these areas, development of the conceptual faculty began in earnest.

The pace of learning at the Rankl Institute was a deliberate one. Teachers took care not to advance to higher, more abstract knowledge, before students had grasped simpler underlying concepts. In the classroom, the lecture method predominated. The teacher controlled each class, especially the flow of material—what was essential and what extraneous.

The goal was to develop the conceptual faculty by teaching students to think. Alek had especially loved history. It showed him, through vivid exploration of the past, that ideas—*principles*—what men and women thought—drove the course of human events. History also showed him ideas that, invariably, were still at work in the world, and every bit as powerful, whether for good or for ill.

Rhee knew all this as she walked beside her nephew down the stairs to Neuron. During her years on Arête, she had been the chief architect of the curriculum later adopted by the renowned Rankl Institute in New York City.

She also knew her nephew possessed a certain personal quality possessed by all Rankl Institute graduates. This was an unquenchable love for learning, as if the exercise of the mind were a joy never to be lost—or denied.

By age fifteen, if not before, most Rankl students had a good sense of where they wanted to take their lives. By then, most were already seasoned explorers. Alek Rankl knew quite young what he wanted. His overriding passion—something he had extensively and deeply explored on his own under the guidance of a favorite science teacher—had long been the world of cyberspace.

"Prodigy" just doesn't do it," a teacher was once heard to say at a faculty meeting, "if you're trying to grasp the potential of Alek Rankl."

At age thirteen, he sat for the entrance exams of the acclaimed New York Academy of Cyberscience. The Academy accepted him as the youngest student in their history. At age sixteen he graduated with a Bachelor of Science in Cyber History and spent another year getting a second degree, in International Cyber Relations. Then at age nineteen with a Master of Science in Cyber Espionage, he was offered a prestigious Henderson Scholarship to continue his studies in Bern Switzerland. The Bern Henderson Institute was the leading center of Cyber Warfare strategy in the West. He was there for more than three years, the third as a coadjutant instructor part time.

It was at that point that his aunt and uncle finally invited Alek to Oribel. Both knew that their nephew would quickly realize for himself why they had waited so long to bring him to Oribel. It was about to happen now.

Neuron was *his* world. All his post Rankl Institute studies prepared him for this place. They had given him the deep knowledge and prodigious skills required to understand what Neuron was about. Most vitally, a mind like his, in the full bloom of youth, was needed, not only to develop it further, but also to identify and remedy vulnerabilities.

Neuron

Alek Rankl entered an expansive chamber. He stopped just inside the entrance, poised there. Rhee had moved off to her office on the right, where she watched from the doorway. His hands hung at his sides and alternately closed into loose fists before opening again. He kept repeating this, as if he were gathering it all in, not only mentally but physically.

It was a cavern-like room, circular and cool, roughly two hundred paces in diameter, and high-ceilinged. A sponge-like pale material clad a continuous wall, blending seamlessly with a slightly curved ceiling. Lighting was a diffused mellow glow emanating from the material itself, creating the effect of soft backlighting. The material also effectively absorbed most white noise.

Visual material streamed onto open wall surfaces around the room. A number of these feeds were quite conventional, such as maps and trend lines, while others were strangely different. Some of these reminded Alek of the neural networks that his parents—both of them neurosurgeons in New York—had on the walls of their home office. But he realized they were not really that. Still others seemed similar to evolutionary trees of bacteria and other ancient life forms that he had always had on his bedroom ceiling, compliments of his great-grandfather, Marek. But these did not quite do it either.

He saw Liang talking and listening and talking again, while interacting with a data display on the ceiling above her head. She momentarily paused when she felt eyes on her, turned, and broke into a radiant smile, before turning back. At another station, Eric was huddled with a lanky older man, strangely familiar, whose shaved head glowed in the soft ambient light. They were discussing what a pulsing display was telling them.

Around the room's perimeter, random patches of wall were illuminated by continually looping text, or formulas, or symbols—*codes*. Eric's associate swiveled his chair and pointed at a nearby wall display. Alek was astonished to see the profile of the man who, before an early retirement, had been the world's leading cyber scientist. As the man swiveled back to Eric, Alek thought he heard him say, "As usual, there's an especially sophisticated biological neural network that has to be untangled."

Alek walked over to the wall and studied the coded network to which the scientist had referred. His uncle came up beside him. "You're looking at an underlying manifestation—coded—of the current threat," he explained to his nephew. "Davesh—yes, I know you recognize Davesh Navendra—uncovered it and brought it to my attention. He expects to unravel it by evening."

Later that morning, Alek, Davesh, and Liang were talking over coffee in the long room. Eric and Rhee, off to the side, watched the scientist ask Alek questions, probing his knowledge. For most answers, he simply nodded, for others, he probed deeper. During an extended response by Alek, Eric noticed the rapt attention on Liang's face. He nudged his wife. "I know," Rhee said under her breath.

They also saw Alek quizzing Navendra, and, a number of times, after hearing the scientist's answer, they saw him turn his head toward a miniature bot, barely visible on his shoulder. This pleased Navendra, for he knew it was a mind-reading device. The turn of head momentarily lined up Alek's frontal cortex with the bot's mind-read function. Most commonly, it would be for a simple mental command, such as, *Save the last minute*, along with a codeword enabling later retrieval, at will, of the desired information.

The young man is impressive, Navendra thought to himself. He not only knows the science, but he also grasps many of the underlying concepts as well. Most impressive are his questions. Not many in the world are supposed to know enough to ask those questions—questions regarding the dark-organic dimension of cyberspace. The organic nature of it yes—that's been around a long time—but not the darkest areas, ones the Frontier has plumbed—and exploited, not in any depth anyway. Then on top of it, I know there are things he can teach me, from his years at Henderson, and, who in the world knows, where else. I must remember to bring my mind-reading bot with me, whenever we're together.

After Liang and Navendra left for Arête, Alek Rankl remained in the room. He walked over to the louvered windows and stood gazing out to Arête on the horizon. He thought about what he had seen and heard—*learned*. He was quietly exhilarated.

IN OUR POWER

It was afternoon of Alek Rankl's third day on Oribel, and as he paused at the entrance to Ventana Garden, he thought of the portals that were still ahead.

From the far end of the garden, he heard the familiar sound of waves heaving against the island's low cliffs, below his line of sight. A breeze stirred the forest foliage, and their shadows played in and out of sunlit patches on the ground. His heightened anticipation from a morning in the Neuron Center mirrored the animation of this place. Ventana was beckoning to him, and standing at its entrance, he pondered the source of its magnetic pull.

The anticipation, he realized, came from his growing awareness that a great venture was underway, a venture that he had been invited to join. There was a certain audacity to it. Yesterday's portal, dramatizing a Declaration of Freedom which would be flung into the face of the world, had made that audacity clear.

He entered the garden and walked to the next portal plate, *In Our Power*. Initiating it, the virtual image of Marek Rankl, still in his middle years, appeared before him again and spoke. *So now that you have gotten to this eighth portal of Ventana Garden, I know you are eager to continue. I know I have gotten your attention. You would not be here with me now unless I had.*

Marek Rankl paused and was so totally concentrated on his great-grandson that Alek imagined that his thoughts were being read and that Marek was saying, *Forget what is in your mind at this moment and pay attention to me for what I am about to say will be life-changing.* Alek listened with a laser sharp focus.

It is now more than three thousand years after the Prometheus myth was first conceived in Ancient Greece. Ever since, this figure has been the great icon of defiance in the world. For the Greeks, especially in Aeschylus's telling, it was defiance in the cause of reason, the same defiance informing our great venture, the Prometheus Frontier. Our Frontier is the last bastion of defiance against the forces of unreason on planet Earth. We do not take this lightly nor do we lightly extend offers to join us. Alek heard the unspoken words in his mind, *Such as the offer you have received.*

Marek Rankl's face had become somber. With his gaze fixed on the young man before him, he overlapped his hands, palms down, and lifted them chin high before his face. His raised elbows were extended out to each side, a bit lower than his hands. Thus poised, his hands and forearms simulated a bridge, and he held it for long moments.

Finally he moved, pushing the bridge forward toward Alek while bowing his head ever so slightly. Through it all, he kept his eyes locked on his great-grandson's. Alek distinctly saw—*felt*—the solemnity of what had just happened. It reminded him of the salute familiar to those trained in the Asian martial arts. Having had that training himself, he spontaneously returned Marek's modification of it, slightly bowing his head in turn, while maintaining eye contact.

He saw a smile light Marek Rankl's face; then his image faded.

But the afterimage of a bridge lingered, and Alek realized that an indelible spiritual link had been established—and then transmitted—between him and the man who had just disappeared into the warm tropical air—the man with the vision of a grand and new and audacious adventure—an adventure known as the Prometheus Frontier.

He has just made me part of that adventure, Alek said to himself, suddenly overwhelmed.

The narrative continued with a new voice, and the visuals switched to another data stream, New York harbor. Pangaia, which began life ten years after Marek Rankl had founded RME, had grown steadily more powerful.

Pangaia had taken a century-old world organization and infused it with the social philosophy of visionary, Herbert Henry. Commentators remarked that Henry had thus made that organization youthful again, even vibrant.

The nations of the world found themselves part of an organization that was different in two important ways. First, it was now fully democratic. Each member state, regardless of size, was equal in stature and had one vote. During his life, Herbert Henry had insisted that egalitarianism and multiculturalism, revered throughout the world, required this. Larger nations are not better simply because of greater size or strength or wealth—and certainly not because of an allegedly richer culture. Typically, larger nations listened politely but ignored it.

Second, for each member nation, Herbert Henry's philosophy was the all-embracing, over-arching authority. He had envisioned nothing less, as one of his "first principles" made clear.

In Our Power

All areas of life, public and private, must be under the control of a central authority—Pangaia

Alek found himself in a convention hall where Henry elaborated before a large audience. "The justification of this principle," he intoned, "is the innate weakness and depravity of human nature. Never has there been an age during which powerful central authority has not been needed to quell the endless rapaciousness of the human animal."

In a great sports arena, Henry explained the principle's scope. "What does *public* mean?" he asked. "*Public* means government, politics, economics, finance, education, and medicine. It means scientific research, internet, trade, commerce, environment, the oceans, space—plus any other human enterprise or arena the future brings."

He did the same with the concept *private*. "*Private*," he declared, "refers to all matters of conscience. It means spirituality, ethics, and morality. It means ideas. It means the mental, the psychological.

"The *public* is the vast realm of human enterprises, while the *private* is the realm of human consciousness and human spirit and human knowledge, the products of which underlie and support and advance human enterprises. For that reason, in terms of fundamentality, the *private* has preeminence."

Herbert Henry's fellow intellectuals typically regarded consciousness as a passive byproduct of the human organism, with no active role in human functioning. But in Henry's world view it was just the reverse. "The immaterial," he was often heard to declare, "by which I mean any product of consciousness, is metaphysically a different stuff. I do not know what that stuff is. Except for God, no one does. But whatever it is, I prefer to regard it as the proper meaning of the concept *spiritual*. It might always remain a mystery, yet it is the one essential force that drives the material realm."

Henry was so convinced that this was so, that he codified it with a principle he designated as *The Primacy of the Immaterial*.

> Seek first to control the spiritual realm, then to control the material.

A commentator once referred to it as "Henry's principle of thought control." This characterization stuck.

Herbert Henry's impact on Pangaia was profound. His social philosophy set the course of the organization, logically driving the causes it championed, as well as those it vilified.

Its ideological organ, the *Pangaia Times*, was vast in its reach, with offices in all the world's major cities. Annually, the *Times* recruited from the best liberal arts schools, paying special attention to graduates who had majored in disciplines such as communication, history, and journalism.

All graduates started employment with six months of indoctrination in the *Times* building on Pangaia Island in New York. The graduates were already well familiar with what the *Times* espoused. They knew it championed the central authority of Pangaia to govern all economic activity. They knew it advanced the role of Pangaia to define a universal system of education to shape the thinking of the young—children who would then become model citizens of the world. They knew the *Times* advanced a social system whose body of laws would govern all sectors of life, public and private, and thus ensure that Pangaia's overarching authority brought about the desired results.

In Our Power

Pangaia the organization regarded its six-month training program vitally important for new recruits of the *Times*. It integrated the knowledge they already possessed with the social philosophy of Herbert Henry. They became more effective champions of Pangaia's causes. More importantly, they became more eloquent vilifiers of any entity opposed to those causes.

Recruits of the *Pangaia Times* reveled in their six months of training. What especially struck them was Herbert Henry's Primacy of the Immaterial principle: control the spiritual to control the material. Their instructors made it clear that, as *Times* employees, they were now on a spiritual mission. Control the minds, the spirits of your enemy and you have the key to controlling them completely. The fact that their cause was spiritual—*sacred*—was an exhilarating realization to young minds. "That's the business we are in," they were told, over and over.

Once again, the visual stream switched, and Alek found himself in Vindauge Tower in New York City. He saw Marek Rankl gazing south to the tip of Manhattan from the great room, one level down from the top of the tower. It was an hour after sunrise, and he was clad in yoga pants and a dark tee shirt.

A soft male voice engaged Alek's ear. Marek had just come from his workout area next to the master bedroom. He was gazing through binoculars at Pangaia Island and saw its gray three-story buildings, each defining a major geographical region. Each region, Marek knew, had been enriched to the extent it traded with Rankl Marine Enterprises.

But he also knew that Pangaia, through its mouthpiece, the *Pangaia Times,* thought otherwise. It viewed RME as its arch enemy, with its unfettered capitalism, its monopoly of Earth's material resources, which rightfully belonged to every nation, and its monopoly of the world's great brains, which rightfully belonged to their nations of origin, where they were most needed. For all these reasons, and many others, RME must be curtailed, and ultimately brought to its knees.

Marek's binoculars moved to the right and stopped on the Statue of Liberty. He saw the mutilated figure, the right arm reduced to a mere stump as a result of the laser attack years earlier. Standing there, he was frozen in time, pondering what evil had made it possible.

"I see where you're looking," Alek heard a voice say.

Marek turned and saw Lenore Pellon, as did Alek, her body clearly visible under a gauzy shift. She stood in bare feet, coffee mug in hand. Angry dark eyes looked past Marek. They looked to the distance, where she knew the mutilated statue stood.

"Yes," he replied. "And I am struck dumb when I ponder it. It makes such a powerful statement, far more than the fact that a world-famous icon has been desecrated and never repaired. But what is it? What am I missing?"

"I think you already know the answer but have lost sight of it. The answer has to do with what the statue's iconic torch stood for. Yes, surely liberty, but more than that is what liberty makes possible. What it makes possible is that which is best in human nature. It unleashes human potential. It unleashes the human mind.

"I have no doubt that, eventually, evidence will be uncovered that Pangaia the organization was behind the mutilation of Lady Liberty. Her arm, and the torch it held up, had to go. The entire world knew this icon, especially Pangaia Island, a mere stone's throw away in New York harbor. Herbert Henry's dictum—*Seek first to control the spiritual realm,* meaning the mind, *then to control the material*—required that that upheld arm be gone."

Marek Rankl stood in silence then, his eyes slowly moving, side to side. The vid-stream panned between Liberty Island, with its mutilated statue, and Pangaia Island with its gray, characterless buildings, and then back to Liberty Island. Alek knew that both he and his great-grandfather were seeing the connection Lenore had made so vivid.

She came up beside Marek then, and together they continued to look south to the harbor. Even without touching, Marek felt her body, warm next to his. "You really did not need me to tell you this," she said.

"Oh, but I did. I certainly did. You are right, I had forgotten. And that is why I need you with me on this adventure, Dr Lenore Pellon.

"In several years, we will surely be inaugurating Arête, as the first island nation of the Prometheus Frontier. And when we do, we will be igniting a real torch for the entire world to see. It will be in the offshore waters of Arête. And it will be a perpetual flame—never to be extinguished.

"With you, Lenore darling, it truly is in our power."

PAINE

Alek Rankl once again started his day in the garden of portals. As he walked to the next station, *Paine*, white longtails, lazily circled overhead, visible through sky windows in the tropical foliage. He thought of his first morning on Oribel Island. These native sea birds had been visible then also. It was as if they were keeping watch—monitoring his progress.

He entered the portal, and he was transported two thousand miles north, and the better part of a century back in time. Once again, he was in the great room near the top of Vindauge Tower in New York City. Marek Rankl and Lenore Pellon were still standing side by side as they gazed down to the harbor in the distance. Alek heard Marek's voice, repeating the final words of the last portal. "With you, Lenore darling, it truly is in our power."

As the scene faded out and spiral stairs came into focus, Alek felt himself transported to the tower's top floor, the eightieth. He saw the conference room and entered. The participants were at a very large square table, with a lectern midpoint along one of its four sides. Opposite the lectern, in the rear of the room, he saw a breakfast buffet next to the floor-to-ceiling windows.

A four-sided hologram dominated the air space above the conference table, visible from any seat in the room. It was displaying a steady stream of visual material that alternated between panoramic exterior views of the city and interior views of the conference room and participants.

Alek recognized Armando Rojas and Lenore Pellon. Each was in conversation with colleagues they were next to at the table. Most of the chairs were occupied, but except for the two he recognized, the faces were unfamiliar. The ambiance was clearly one of expectation, accentuated by the unfilled champagne flutes standing like soldiers around the table.

Alek felt himself drawn to an empty chair. It conformed to his body as he sat, and he found himself directly facing the lectern on the opposite side of the spacious table.

As if he had been waiting for Alek's arrival, Marek Rankl entered the room and went directly to the lectern. He wore a dark shirt with sleeves rolled to his elbows. Scanning the table, he saw more than two dozen faces and said, "I see that everyone is present, including someone who has joined us virtually." To Alek's utter astonishment, he saw his great-grandfather's eyes meet his and hold them momentarily.

After his welcome greeting, Marek said, "We all know why we are here this morning. Over the years, each of you, in various venues—often one-on-one with me, sometimes in meetings—has explored a vision. That vision is the *Prometheus Frontier*.

"As we explored it, we informally referred to ourselves as the *Paine* group, or simply, *Paine*. The time has come to make it formal. Today we officially charter the *Paine Society*. But before we do that," he said, looking up to the hologram, "let us consider the milestones that got us to where we are this morning."

FRONTIER MILESTONES

Rankle Marine Enterprises
Foundation
Declaration of Freedom
Arête Acquisition

"Rankl Marine Enterprises started life a quarter of a century ago. Over the years, our magnificent growth, no matter how well earned, has only provoked ever-increasing hostility in the world. And that hostility has brought with it ever-increasing onslaughts of coercion against RME and our trading partners. These onslaughts gradually led to the formation of a vision, a vision we all know as the Prometheus Frontier.

"As this vision took shape, I took it to RME's board of directors and, as everyone in this room knows, the vision generated excitement. Rankl Marine Enterprises created a legal entity, the Frontier Foundation, soon known simply as the *Foundation*, with bylaws to govern all Frontier activity going forward.

"But philosophy has always been a great passion for me, and for quite some time, I have worked to formulate a philosophic Declaration of Freedom. By freedom, I mean political freedom. That is, I mean freedom from initiated physical force—initiated physical coercion—from *any* quarter, public or private.

"Fortunately, in the final stages of formulating a Declaration of Freedom, I had a professional philosopher with me, our very own Lenore Pellon. All of you have seen the Declaration in its final form. Its importance cannot be overemphasized. It is our seminal founding document—our vision, our inspiration, our rallying cry. In short, without it, the Prometheus Frontier would not even get off the ground.

"Then, shortly after, we closed on the acquisition of Arête. This was the fourth milestone in the realization of our vision.

"Today we reach a fifth milestone. Today the Foundation takes our informal Paine group and officially charters the Paine *Society*. So let us proceed."

Marek Rankl paused for long moments before beginning. "Three hundred years ago," he said, "Thomas Paine's rallying cry to America's thirteen original colonies was: *We have it in our power to begin the world over again.* We excerpt the charter of the Paine Society from that cry," he said, glancing at the hologram.

THE PAINE SOCIETY

To begin the world
over again

"Each person in this room, as of this moment, is a charter member of the Paine Society. And that includes our virtual guest," he said, as his eyes found Alek's again.

"Each person in this room is hereby chartered—*charged*—to begin the world over again. Through Paine, we will bring the Prometheus Frontier into concrete existence. It will happen with the inauguration of Arête as the Frontier's first island nation. That inauguration will be our next crucial milestone and will happen inside of the next ten years.

"But the lifespan of Paine will not end with that inauguration. My vision for Paine, the *Foundation's* vision, is that the Paine Society will exist in perpetuity, as the Prometheus Frontier grows and expands. As the number of island states increases, the Frontier will become a federation of islands. But the role of Paine will remain unchanged. Its charter is perpetual. And its importance, its vital role, will only increase as the Frontier grows.

"Congratulations to you all!" said Marek Rankl, as he led the applause which then filled the room. Everyone was standing. He paused as servers filled the champagne flutes, and soon there was one in every hand. Holding his glass aloft, Marek said, "To begin the world over again." All in the room followed his lead and held their glasses toward him as they said, "To begin the world over again." But before he drank, they saw Marek turn to his right and touch his glass to Lenore Pellon's and then to his left, to Armando Rojas's. Before drinking, each person did the same with those they were next to, and the room filled with the shimmering music of crystal on crystal.

Everyone remained standing—caught up in the excitement of what had just transpired—all of them struck by the tribute they had received from a man who meant so much to them—Marek Rankl. Each of them was a founding member of a Society—*Paine*—which was to endure into perpetuity.

They heard his voice call their attention to a dark wooden table, highly polished, being wheeled into the room. It held an amber-toned parchment, on the surface of which, ornate calligraphic lettering seemed to be all but dancing—a spinning, swirling dance on the stage of history. Three word groupings made clear that the document had three distinct sections. To complete this tableau, a long white quill with a golden nib rested beside an inkwell of heavy crystal.

Then he announced, "Each of you will now affix your name to the bottom of this document, below the text. I will be the last to sign, but other than that, there is no particular order."

One by one, each person dipped into the ink, selected a spot at random, signed, and passed the quill. Finally, Marek Rankl signed. It was done. All in the room stood around the table, looking down upon it. Twenty-five names filled the bottom border of the document. Each signature was distinctive—some dramatically so.

On the top border, the header fairly leapt out from the parchment.

DECLARATION OF FREEDOM
The Prometheus Frontier

RANKL'S FOLLY

After the celebratory break, Marek Rankl returned to the lectern. This would be his first address to the newly chartered Paine Society.

"Ever since we expressed interest in the sovereign island of Arête," he started, "skeptics and naysayers have referred to it as *Rankl's Folly*. Skeptics ask: Why begin over when liberty groups throughout the world successfully pursue that goal incrementally. That is, through gradual incremental progress, *not* through a revolutionary restart.

"Naysayers ask a different question: Why begin over when so many have already tried and failed. Remember floating nations and seasteading and other new ventures which have been shut down by the powers that be. Those powers can be internal, neighboring, or even distant. Regarding that last, even the sniff of a threat can cause venture capital to dry up.

"Both skeptics and naysayers are asking what I refer to as *The Big Why*. And with venture capital so vitally important, it is essential that we fully understand why skeptics and naysayers are wrong. Lenore Pellon will hold forth on that subject this morning."

———

As Lenore approached the lectern, the hologram's header changed to *Progress: Incremental & Revolutionary*. "I want to start," she began, "by making two general points about incremental progress, points that talk directly to the skeptic view." As always, her resonant, musical voice commanded immediate attention.

"First, incremental progress is a good thing. Incremental progress toward a fully free society is vitally important. It preps the way, buys time, and maintains the fire while a society marshals its resources for beginning over afresh, should that, in fact, be its eventual goal. Whether it is or not, we should support incremental progress whenever and wherever we see it. It is the right thing to do. That is point number one.

"Second, incremental progress is not enough to accomplish a fully free society. Such a gigantic goal requires gigantic steps—*revolutionary* steps. That's point number two.

"Now I want you to consider how history illustrates this," she said, glancing up. The hologram enlarged to display a two-thousand-year timeline. *Human Progress* was its title. Time in hundred-year increments was on the horizontal axis, and living standard was plotted on the vertical.

"Observe," she said, "that for nearly all this time, the line was flat. And we know from history that this flat line represented a living standard at the bare subsistence level, as the timeline notes. Even after the Dark Ages, the line basically remained flat at that subsistence level.

"There was improvement of course. People were living longer, and there were more of them. Infant mortality decreased, as medical and scientific knowledge increased. But these advances and many others did not really reflect significant growth. The progress that occurred was *incremental* progress. It was relatively small.

Rankl's Folly

"But look at the mid-eighteenth century. The living standard jumped to a dramatically higher level and never regressed. The industrial revolution had occurred, driven by intellectual giants engaged in the processes of thinking and invention.

"These giants were building on the scientific revolution. They took scientific laws and applied them to address human needs. The steam engine was a vivid example. It was the steam engine that powered the first locomotives and steamboats and factories of all kinds. Likewise, an explosion of other inventions vastly increased the efficiency of human work. The historical evidence is undeniable. During earlier centuries, there was steady incremental improvement overall, but it took revolutions to drive revolutionary improvement.

"Whether we look at living standard or at freedom or at any other measure of human progress, it has been revolution sparked by great minds, *not* small incremental steps, which has produced great change. History illustrates that reality.

"The revolutionary charter of the Paine Society is in that tradition and makes each of us in this room a revolutionary."

After a short break, Alek returned to his seat and found that someone had brought him coffee and an egg sandwich. He paused, not sure where the virtual ended and the real began. But he found the simple fare to be real—and delicious.

Lenore was again at the lectern. "So much for the skeptics," she said, "for the notion that a complete restart is unnecessary because incremental progress *makes* it unnecessary.

"Now, let's consider the naysayers. The naysayers come at it differently. They believe that a restart is at best foolish and at worst insane. The challenges are *that* formidable. I'm going to advance a number of reasons, however, in ascending order of importance, why that belief, in *any* form, is wrong." She looked up.

WHAT NAYSAYERS IGNORE

Human Potential
Real Estate
Venture Capital
Defense
Philosophy

"Naysayers ignore five key considerations," she stated, "and human potential is the first. At any one time, around the globe, mankind's best is ever watching for the next land of unlimited opportunity. They are looking for a land where they can pursue their dreams and advance their lives. And, in doing so, they advance the nations to which they have fled.

"Tragically, all too often, immigration is not managed well. But on Arête, especially in the early years of the Besosa era, it *was*, thanks to Angel and Livia Ramos. They will be telling us about it today.

"*Real Estate* is next. Impoverished islands exist in abundance around the world, silently crying for rescue, begging to be lifted out of impoverishment."

A woman's voice, next to Armando, called out, "Arête!"

Lenore looked to her left and said, "Yes, Livia, you and Angel know that better than anyone else in this room."

Rankl's Folly

Alek, seeing the exchange, now realized that, earlier, Armando had been talking to Angel and Livia Ramos, the husband-and-wife team that so successfully ran Arête's immigration program during the early Besosa regime. Livia's hair was starting to turn, while Angel's remained full and mostly black, but with a striking shock of white above his right temple.

"Next: *Venture Capital,*" Lenore continued. Around the world, venture capitalists exist in great numbers, and since RME's acquisition of Arête, there has been intense interest from them. The reputation of Rankl Marine Enterprises was the only collateral needed.

"And now, *Defense.* Defense is without doubt the greatest risk factor in the eyes of the nay-sayer. How will Arête survive in an ever-hostile world," they ask. "We have just talked about the abundance of human potential, real estate, and venture capital in the world at large. But what good are these without the ability to defend them against initiated physical force, in whatever form it might take.

"But Rankle Marine Enterprises has not become an industrial giant without a strong defense system. That defense system will be ever more effective by the time we inaugurate Arête as the first nation state of the Prometheus Frontier.

"Finally, there is *Philosophy*. Far and away, philosophy is the most vital consideration ignored by nay-sayers. Philosophy has given us our vision. Philosophy provides the intellectual foundation which makes possible the actualization of that vision. And philosophy gives us the ability to ensure its long-term flourishing. In a word, philosophy is power.

"The philosophy of which I speak animates our Declaration of Freedom and as Marek has stressed, without the Declaration, the Prometheus Frontier would not even get off the ground. And with that, I want to give back the lectern to Marek."

Rankl's Folly

"I would like to summarize what we have so far," Marek Rankl said. "Five considerations, taken together, make for a compelling case that there has never been a more auspicious time for beginning the world over again. I want to emphasize this in a single statement."

He slowed his words, and the hologram displayed them one line at a time, to accentuate them even further.

> To begin the world over again—now—
> involves tapping into and developing
> what already exists in great abundance:
>
> Human Potential
> Real Estate
> Venture Capital
> Defense Capability
> A Powerful Philosophy

"Now here is what I find especially exciting," he declared. "Consider the implications of all this. With all these resources available to us at this time, still early in the third millennium, creating a totally free society through beginning over again is indeed vastly easier, and faster, than seeking to achieve it through incremental change alone.

"But it does not stop with that. After the Frontier has launched and started to flourish, it will have a catalytic effect. It will accelerate incremental progress around the globe. It will do this in a very powerful way: the persuasive power of an already-existing example. The Frontier will provide evidence that a totally free and flourishing society is possible."

Rankl's Folly

Marek paused briefly and said, "Before we break for lunch, let us re-cap what we have done this morning and identify priorities.

"This morning, we—all of us in this room—became charter members of the Paine Society. Our charter is to begin the world over again. And our goal is to initiate this restart within ten years, with the inauguration of Arête as the first island nation of the Prometheus Frontier.

"At this point, we are at a critical stage, and the work ahead of us is challenging. Yes, we saw this morning that the time is right and the necessary resources for success exist in abundance. And yes, we have the all-important Declaration of Freedom to define our philosophy going forward.

"But it is one thing to have a vision and quite another to execute on that vision. Despite all the resources, when we look at today's world, the Prometheus Frontier could, nonetheless, readily be seen as utterly audacious and unrealistic.

"But this means only one thing. It means that it is absolutely essential for us clearly to identify our greatest priorities. Not that we have not been prioritizing up to now. We have always done that. But now, it is order-of-magnitude more important.

"And thus, do we arrive at our final agenda item: *Priorities*. During the lunch break, I want each of you to consider the above provisional priority list, for discussion after lunch."

PROVISIONAL PAINE PRIORITIES

Constitution and Government
Infrastructure
Defense

Rankl's Folly

"Consider these priorities and ask whether they capture what is most essential now. And ask whether they sufficiently take into account the state of the world at large."

PRIORITIES

During lunch, Alek watched and listened, as discussion of priorities intermixed with trips to the buffet table. At one point he found that, again, a plate had been prepared for him. Finally, Marek returned to the lectern, and looking up to the hologram, solicited inputs regarding the proposed Paine priorities.

PAINE SOCIETY PRIORITIES

Constitution and Government
Infrastructure
Defense

Livia Ramos was the first to speak. "I want to suggest a further priority, one that is easy to take for granted but potentially relates to *any* priority. It has to do with something you talked about this morning—human potential. For quite some time, Angel and I have been in the business of human capital, closely related to human potential. We'd like to go on the agenda and present a few of our thoughts."

"Done," Marek stated, as the hologram changed, "especially since it potentially relates to any priority. You and Angel will be up first."

The next input was an observation from Karen McTeague, one of RME's marine microbiologists. "Constitution and Government,

Priorities

taken together, sounds a bit ambitious. Shouldn't they be handled separately?" she asked.

"That was our thinking originally," Marek replied, "but the more we thought about it, the more we realized that constitution and government would be best handled together. They are closely intertwined, and our government's size will probably be a small fraction of what technologically advanced countries typically have."

A deep gravelly voice was next. All eyes went to Art Haag, a large gray-haired man. Haag had long led RME's New Venture Division as well as the Frontier Foundation.

Haag was an unerring judge of prospective investors, from the standpoint of whether they would fit Rankl's culture and vision. His wife, Judith Barry, an industrial engineer by trade, with an advanced degree in reliability engineering, possessed an uncanny ability to identify, whatever the venture, areas most in need of risk mitigation.

"Judith and I," he began, "would suggest replacing *Infrastructure* with *Foundation*. The role of the Frontier's Foundation cannot be overemphasized as we go forward. From a financial standpoint, nothing happens without its involvement, and of course that includes infrastructure. We believe it would be good to emphasize the fundamental role of the Foundation."

"I agree," said Marek, and looking up, Alek again saw the agenda change.

PAINE SOCIETY PRIORITIES

Human Capital/Potential
Constitution and Government
The Frontier Foundation
Defense

103

Marek then stated that the afternoon would cover the first three items, but that defense, a huge area, would need at least a day of its own. He then turned the lectern over to Livia Ramos.

———

"Human Capital," Livia started, "is the ultimate resource in any new venture. Every step rests upon it. Human capital is the knowledge, talent, even street smarts, possessed by individuals seeking to advance that venture.

Knowledge possessed by individuals might be limited; talents might be modest. Everyone is different, *individual*. But everyone's input is vital. It's an attitude and a fire in the belly that I'm talking about. Knowledge and ability, in whatever form or degree they express themselves, comprise the currency by which society advances and flourishes. Knowledge, understood in this way, truly is the ultimate resource.

"Angel and I are remembered for managing a successful immigration program, early in the Jorge Besosa era. But, actually, it was part of a *Human Capital* program. We were in the business of attracting, and then paving the way for people who were self-motivated—self-starters.

"For a number of decades Besosa's Arête flourished. We attracted immigrants possessing the fire I mentioned—the intense desire to better their lives, their families, and themselves. We were able to give them an environment which unleashed—indeed, *welcomed* their spark, and gave them opportunity to grow. It was a golden age for Arête. But it did not last. Free enterprise, a cause that Besosa himself supported initially, gradually waned as government intervention in private enterprises gradually increased.

Priorities

"Later, with the acquisition of our island by RME, and our immediate engagement with the Foundation, Angel and I realized that re-vitalization was on Arête's horizon. There were two indications of this. First, we saw that RME was an organization which holds education sacred—a key element of its corporate culture. Second, and nearly as important, we knew the Foundation saw the enormous potential of Arête as a retirement mecca.

"Angel and I were thrilled when we realized that an even greater potential was taking shape. Consider the vast reservoir of knowledge waiting to be tapped in any retirement population. Consider further, the unlimited curiosity for knowledge in the youth of any culture. And, further still, consider the ways those two realities could intersect, mesh—be *integrated*. The potential is limited only by one's imagination."

Livia and Angel Ramos needed to say no more. The room came alive with excitement. For several minutes animated voices explored the possibilities. Finally, Marek's voice brought discussion to a conclusion. "The Foundation," he informed the room, "will be establishing a Department of Human Capital within its walls, headed by Angel and Livia Ramos. Its charter will be simple: Make Arête an educational mecca, renowned for its excellence.

Lenore was next at the lectern, to present Constitution and Government. "Upon completion of the Declaration of Freedom," she started, "Marek, Jon Ripley, and I put our heads together to plan the next step. Jon Ripley," she reminded the audience, "is a marine agronomist with an intense interest in philosophy—especially the branch of philosophy known as politics, which studies the nature and proper function of government.

Priorities

Philosophy was Jon's minor at Ocean Polytechnic; he was one of my students.

"By the time Jon joined Marek and me, the Frontier's political philosophy had been set forth in the Declaration of Freedom. We had also proclaimed that the form of our government would be a Constitutional Republic. We now had to frame that government and then, flesh it out—that is, define how Arête's new government would actually work.

"The basic framework is what you see above," she said, looking up to the hologram.

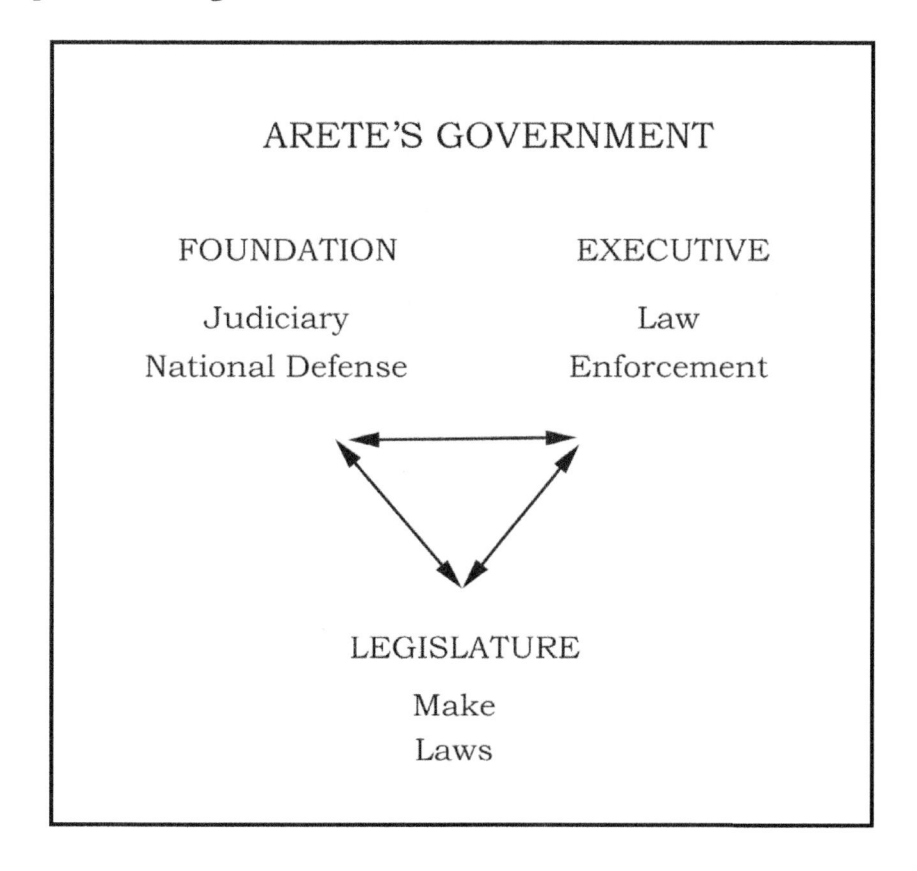

ARETE'S GOVERNMENT

FOUNDATION	EXECUTIVE
Judiciary	Law
National Defense	Enforcement

LEGISLATURE

Make
Laws

Priorities

"The Foundation has the judicial system, including the highest court. It also has national defense. The Executive branch has law enforcement, while the Legislature makes the laws.

"Two general points apply to this basic framework. First, animating each branch is the Declaration of Freedom. The Declaration is the soul of Arête's government and the preamble to the constitution. And second, checks and balances exist by virtue of the fact that the three branches are in continuous dynamic interaction. The three sets of double-pronged arrows capture that.

"In summary, this is the bare framework, the skeleton. Now we need to flesh it out. This will happen in the coming ten years, before inauguration."

After a short break, Jon Ripley took the lectern. He was a tall, intense man with a trimmed beard. Looking up to the hologram, he stated, "In fleshing out this basic framework, the Constitution and Government team started by identifying what types of issues faced us.

This is what we started with," he said, as the hologram changed.

```
CONSTITUTIONAL ISSUES

        General
     Nuts and Bolts
         Rights
       Adjudication
        Language
      Slippery Slopes
```

Priorities

"Before I begin, he said, I want to make clear that, for each group, I'm only going to give you a small sampling of a larger population of issues. But it will give you an idea of what's in each category." Alek watched and listened, with great interest.

For *General* issues, Ripley elaborated on human reason as the ultimate authority in any legitimate government and the fact that, even with reason, honest disagreements will arise and mistakes made. Humans are not infallible. Of course, these realities exist in all three government branches, as well as for their interactions—just as they do in any human interaction.

For *Nuts and Bolts,* he discussed government funding, government service, and the role and nature of political parties in a free society. He pointed out that volunteerism in government service is another area, like education, in which Angel and Livia's intellectual capital program will no doubt engage.

Rights, what they are and how they get violated is a complex area, Ripley pointed out to his audience. There are rights such as life, liberty, property, and the pursuit of happiness; there are intellectual property rights. There is the fact that only initiated physical force violates rights. What constitutes physical force and what does not, can be tricky. Is a verbal insult physical force? If yes, then what about the right of free speech?

Regarding *Adjudication,* Ripley indicated some of the questions with which they were grappling. If adjudicators are appointed, who does the appointing? What does the ratification process look like? Are there term limits? And what about Arête's retirement population? Is there any reason not to engage the island's elders, as will surely be happening with education?

Language is vital in so much of what we do, Ripley pointed out next. He reminded his audience of constitutional battles in history, where disastrous outcomes could have been averted, had key passages initially been formulated with uncompromising, explicit language, not open to interpretation.

For *Slippery Slope* dangers, Ripley cited an example he learned from Lenore. If a constitution's framers fail to explicitly prohibit government intervention in the economy, the nation is put on a slippery slope to rampant cronyism and fiscal constituencies—that portion of a nation's population largely, even *totally* dependent on government. Centuries of data, from many nations and cultures, provide the evidence.

At this point, Alek heard Ripley ask for questions and comments. Someone asked how the transition from the Besosa government to the new one was going? He responded that, of necessity, Arête's police, judiciary, and defense departments were maintained after the acquisition of Arête, but of course would undergo change with time, by streamlining what was already there, or changing it in some way. But all other legacy departments of the Besosa years—education, medical care, science, and many others—would be gradually privatized. "The aim is to have most transitions completed by inauguration," Ripley stated.

"Talk to us about the indigent, those who really have fallen on hard times?" someone asked. "They are with us, not through any fault of their own; they are unfortunate casualties of the Besosa era."

"The Prometheus Frontier is very concerned to adequately address all legacy wrongs," Jon Ripley replied. "This is the bailiwick of the Foundation, and I'm going to defer to Art Haag, who is about to come up. He'll talk to such issues. One thing for sure, those who have suffered under the later years of Besosa will find their lives and their prospects greatly improved in the Prometheus Frontier."

Priorities

In conclusion, Ripley indicated that defining the Frontier's constitution and government in the coming years will no doubt require many drafts. Even the basic framework of government, as so far defined, might be modified. "We will depend on all Frontier founders, that means all of us gathered here today, to review everything—drafts, trials, corrections—as we go forward.

After a short break, Art Haag was at the lectern. "As you saw earlier," he began, "five milestones mark our journey to the full realization of the Prometheus Frontier: Rankl Marine Enterprises, the Frontier Foundation, Declaration of Freedom., Arête Island, and Paine Society. The sixth will be Inauguration.

"Of course, Marek Rankl never thought the founding of RME was a milestone on a journey to the founding of a new island nation in the stunningly beautiful Caribbean Sea. But it has, and here we are. Each of us is a fortunate part of it." Someone started applauding, and it quickly spread through the room.

Then Haag continued. "The Foundation, my bailiwick, has priorities of its own," he stated, "and this is what they look like."

FOUNDATION PRIORITIES

Besosa Legacy Issues
Property Management
RME Consolidation
Defense Systems

Haag started right in on *Besosa Legacy Issues*. These had to be resolved before the Frontier's acquisition of Arête could go forward. Poverty was widespread, Housing and healthcare facilities were damaged by hurricane and left unrepaired. Opportunity had withered. Education was suffering from shortage of teachers and basic supplies. Medical insurance for most Arêteans was nonexistent.

Arête's once-vibrant cottage industry was struggling. A native population with a long tradition of self-reliance could not compete with the cronyism of the late Besosa years. There was also a certain amount of corruption. Government intervention into private affairs, which had crept in much earlier, no matter how well-intentioned initially, had become a slippery slope to these evils. Government intervention into the private sector always does, Haag pointed out.

Such wrongs had to be righted before acquisition. Often victims received financial compensation, negotiated as to amount, between Besosa and the Frontier. This included wrongs having to do with property rights.

With the mention of "property," Haag easily segued to the challenges of *Property Management* on the island. Arête, upon acquisition by RME, had become a large private island, one hundred miles east to west. Its social system was full capitalism, meaning all property would be privately owned. A large array of legal and financial mechanisms, including trusts, was required to manage the complexities of the various relationships, while protecting the property rights of all concerned. Island infrastructure and common areas were part of that mix, a complex part.

The Frontier's first major infrastructure project was the seawall around Arête City—a project that shaped its very character. Alek had gotten a glimpse of it, upon his arrival in Arête a few nights ago.

Priorities

Now, Haag let a holographic visual stream do the talking, incrementally taking Alek's eyes through a progressive, visual development: the seawall itself, its ladders and rough stairs down to docks and small marinas, to yachts and pleasure craft. Above, there was the long esplanade, with shops and cafes and galleries which ended at the island's eastern tip, while the esplanade curved around an acoustic shell and concert stage.

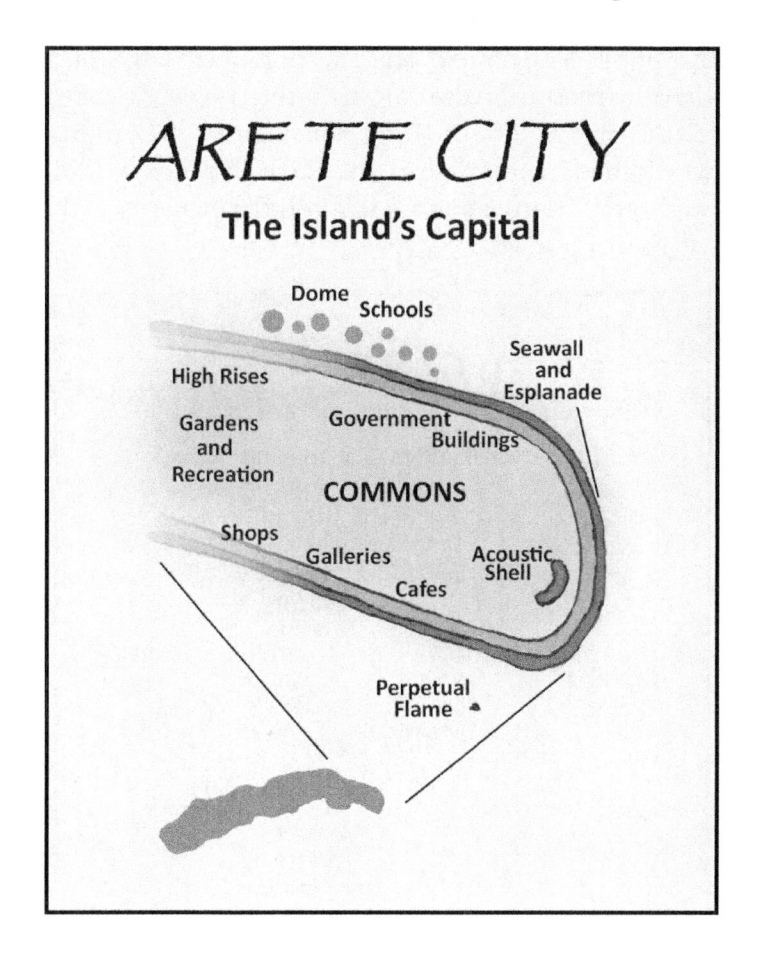

ARETE CITY
The Island's Capital

- Dome
- Schools
- High Rises
- Seawall and Esplanade
- Gardens and Recreation
- Government Buildings
- COMMONS
- Shops
- Galleries
- Cafes
- Acoustic Shell
- Perpetual Flame

Priorities

As it continued along the northern coast of Arête City, larger structures appeared. Haag's voice resumed to explain that these building had a variety of functions, among them government, administration, medical, and scientific. Geodesic structures on manmade islands in the offshore waters, were to be Arête's Dome schools.

The video sequence continued westward, and Alek saw high rises take shape. They lined the far northern edge of the city's coast and continued into the forest, after the esplanade ended.

Before the stream faded, Haag pointed out that many retirees to Arête would live in the high rises. RME families would likewise make them home, many seeking to avail themselves of the nearby schools for their children.

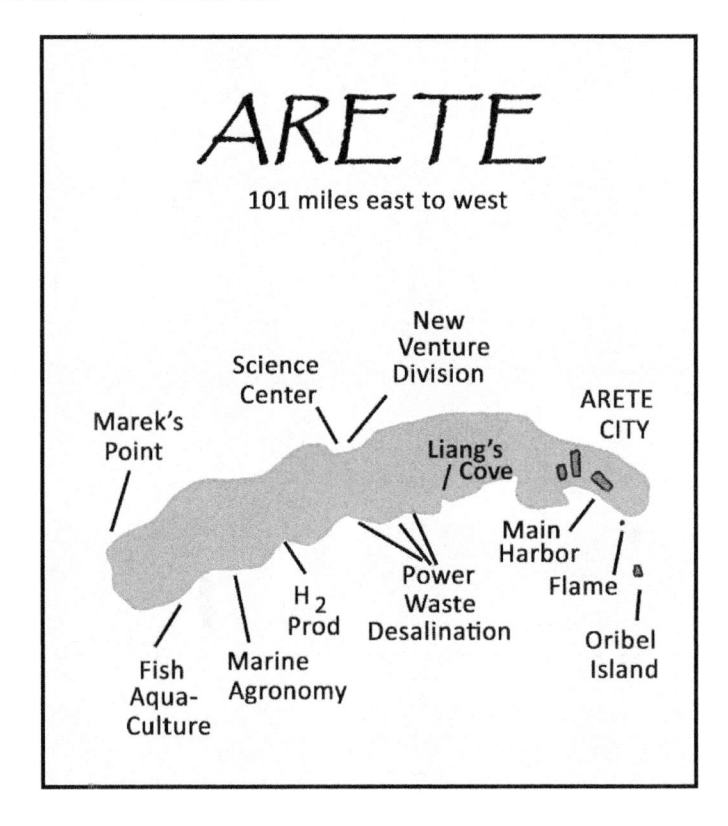

ARETE

101 miles east to west

- New Venture Division
- Science Center
- Marek's Point
- ARETE CITY
- Liang's Cove
- Main Harbor
- Flame
- Power Waste Desalination
- H_2 Prod
- Fish Aqua-Culture
- Marine Agronomy
- Oribel Island

Priorities

RME Consolidation, Haag informed the room, was far and away, the most ambitious priority item prior to inauguration. "Each of our three business enterprises would relocate to Arête," he explained. "The Fish Aquaculture and Marine Agronomy divisions would be located on Arête's southwestern coast, and the New Venture division would be centrally located on the northern coast."

"This consolidation of three major divisions onto one island," Haag pointed out, "will serve two purposes. First, it will enable enhanced integration of our already well-integrated, though diverse enterprises. Second, it will vastly advance our security. Defense, as we all know, is a major consideration—as always."

The mention of defense brought Art Haag to *Defense Systems,* his last agenda item, "Some time ago," he started, "with the Prometheus Frontier already a vision on the horizon, the Foundation chartered various teams to advance RME's already-extensive defense system.

"The Frontier," he concluded, "exponentially increases RME's vulnerabilities. Addressing them has been a massive undertaking, but it is well under way. I think you will find the next two days most interesting."

THE IMMORTALS

Alex left the portal garden and made his way to the lift. He felt charged by the heightened reality of the world he had just left—a world gradually taking shape in order to realize a vision: the Prometheus Frontier.

On the landing pad near the lift, there were three air vehicles. One of them was Liang's, and he realized how much he had been looking forward to seeing her again. He went up to prepare for the evening.

When he arrived in the long room, it was aglow with the late afternoon sun. He saw Rhee, alone in the kitchen area. A large pitcher of sangria stood on a counter. Seven stemmed glasses were next to it, along with two bottles, one a brandy and the other a tropical liqueur. Each bottle had a chrome spout.

Small portable tables at various chairs in the room confirmed that the evening gathering would be a party of seven. Alek noticed the buffet table, on which wooden plates were stacked. He could see that the plates were the same as the ones on which his meals had been served in the portal presentation. "Now I know where my food came from today," he said to Rhee. "And thank you also for matching what was being served in the conference room. It further augmented the reality of it all for me."

Rhee smiled, "I knew you'd appreciate that."

"But what really amazed me was how real my great-grandfather has been, not just today, but in other portals in which he appeared as well. It started with his welcome greeting on the first morning. Then twice today, I could swear his eyes deliberately found mine and held them, as he spoke from the lectern. It was hard to believe that Marek is not really alive."

"But he really *is* alive," a familiar voice behind him said, "in real flesh and in real blood."

"And so am I," a second voice behind him said. It was a familiar woman's voice—Lenore's.

When he spun around, Alek was struck speechless. He saw Marek Rankl and Lenore Pellon. They appeared to be in early middle age, their style of dress essentially what he had seen in the portals. Their hair was much the same as well. He immediately realized they must be virtual figures, fully capable of interacting with real life figures, as Marek did today when he had twice locked eyes with him in the portal. Alek knew this was simply a more sophisticated virtual-real interaction. Truly it was another manifestation of the marvelous flexibility of holo-lasic technology.

Marek, observing his great-grandson's stunned silence, knew what must be in his mind and that he needed to convince him otherwise. He took Lenore's hand and they walked up to Alek. Each of them reached out to him with the hand that was free. "Take our hands," Marek ordered.

And all three of them joined hands to form a circle, in what was to Alek the most exhilarating experience of his young life. He flung his head back and still holding the hands of Marek and Lenore, he looked up to the ceiling. He remained there for long moments, suspended in time, his eyes clenched shut, before allowing himself to be overcome by the prolonged laughter that was demanding to be released.

The Immortals

Davesh, Liang, and Eric entered the room, having come up from the Neuron Center. Rhee poured out seven glasses. Then, brandy bottle in one hand, liqueur bottle in the other, she simultaneously upended them over each drink. When everyone had a glass, Marek lifted his, and looking at Alek, said, "To Alek Rankl, my beloved great-grandson, who has crossed a bridge into the world of Prometheus and is now one of us." Then all in the room lifted their glasses and said in unison, "To Alek Rankl."

Alek found Liang in front of him and saw the radiant animation of her face. Then Rhee announced that the buffet was ready.

Alek was the center of attention that evening. During the day he had become a member of the Paine Society. Marek had made that clear. Twice in today's portal, he had deliberately sought out Alek's eyes and locked onto them.

During the evening, Alek fielded questions from his aunt and uncle, from Lenore, and from Liang. Rhee and Eric sought feedback from Alek regarding the effectiveness of the portals. Were they right, they asked, to tell Marek, earlier than any of them had anticipated, that he was ready to accept the great invitation.

Alek remembered Marek's bridge salute two mornings ago, and his own return of it. He assured them they were right. Any generational gulf that might have stood between him and his great-grandfather had been well bridged. The seven portals he had already been through saw to that.

Lenore and Liang discussed the intellectual defense of the Frontier, and Alek was thrilled to hear that Liang was involved in both hard *and* soft defense. He realized it meant that they would be working together, perhaps even closer than he had thought.

Liang had become fascinated with the microbial foundation of the Neuron Center and all that happened there. She went back to school to expand her knowledge, and Marek himself guided much of her study. Over time, he lent her all his favorite texts, replete with their extensive annotations, in his hand.

Liang had been born on Arête. Both her parents, Taiwanese journalists, had fled there after years in prison. They had committed the folly of thinking they could successfully preserve their island's sovereignty against a great superpower, bent on taking possession of the entire South China Sea.

Later she realized that, although her father had originally received a life sentence, his tortured body had been released after ten years, to serve as a visual warning to other rebels. The sight of his twisted limbs led to Liang's personal vow to commit her life to battling the evil that makes such horror possible.

The following morning, Alek found his great-grandfather alone in the long room, gazing at Armando Rojas's watercolor on the rear wall. He had already run the numbers in his head and knew that Marek now had to be more than 130 years of age.

"Eric told me the story behind this painting and of Armando's other artistic endeavors," he said.

"Yes, Armando Rojas is a great artist and the most important person in my life, after Lenore. He is my closest friend." Alek remained silent. Looking at Marek's face, he knew that his great-grandfather was suddenly elsewhere, lost in memories of an earlier time.

During his early years, Armando spent time on many of the Caribbean's 7000 islands. His mother, Celia Rojas, never married, and Armando never knew his father.

Grandfather Rojas, however, Celia's father, was a great influence. It was from him that Armando first learned to revere honesty, integrity, and self-sufficiency. "Nothing is more important in a man's soul, Mando, than these virtues," he taught his grandson. "You must always remember that."

From his mother he learned a different lesson, but it was one which was equally formative. "First, my son, you must always observe, *really* focus—*see*—the way things are," she would tell him. "Then you must decide what you need to accept, as inescapably given, or have the courage to change, if and when that is necessary."

Celia Rojas was a musician and composer. She was a guitar virtuoso, known throughout the Caribbean and then the world at large, for the poetry she wrote and then put to music. No one alive created melodies as infectiously memorable and haunting. Concert tours over her long life took her to much of the world, as well as a great many of the Caribbean islands. Her young son often accompanied her.

Armando grew up grounded and centered. Like his mother, Celia, he was self-possessed, and she early noticed that, to an extraordinary degree, he emanated an unshakable calm. Even animals sensed this, something of which Celia became aware when he was only eleven. One windy day she watched him swim out to a whale bellowing in the choppy water, as if calling for help. For days it had been dragging a long train of tangled fishing gear and buoys. A woman said, "Can't anyone do something?" and another voice said, "Much too rough and dangerous."

But Armando had already plunged into the water. Seeing the boy, the whale became even more agitated. But Armando set to work gentling the creature, softly sweeping his hands over its head, eyes, and nose. Slowly, the creature quieted. Over the next half hour, Armando untangled it. His bloody hands then returned to the animal's head and, face to face, they looked into each other's eyes. Finally, they separated. The huge creature curled its body into the waves and swam off. But a hundred yards out, it surfaced and looked back. Its final call was a haunting prehistoric sound, before it disappeared into the deep.

In his early teens, Armando became fascinated with the martial arts, a fascination which was to endure for his entire life. He was amazed by what was possible to the unaided human body—the so-called "empty hand." It could be the blazing speed of a back fist, or the levitating power of the unaided human body, or the superhuman strength of a mother lifting a truck off her child, in the middle of a road.

He traveled the islands of his youth seeking out masters of the many extant martial arts. Invariably, they befriended the boy, struck by his dark-haired beauty and earnest enthusiasm. They taught him all they knew, and just as important, they *untaught* his bad habits.

He learned the strengths and weaknesses of each martial art. He studied numerous pressure points—highly vulnerable points of the human body and selected those he could see were most effective and accessible, depending on the situation. Then he practiced, under controlled conditions, until striking or kicking or pressuring them became second nature. He fully realized, for the first time, how deadly the empty hand can be in life-or-death situations.

He also learned how easy it is to render a menacing opponent harmless, simply by grabbing the pinky finger and twisting so that the wrist and then whole body was taken to the ground, with no permanent damage. He competed in pan-Caribbean martial art festivals and became known for his lightning-like speed and the clean precision of his moves.

In his sixteenth year he discovered a fighting art he had not seen before. He was on an unfamiliar island, and a short distance from town, he saw hand to hand fighting being taught on the beach. Men and women, whose light protective gear indicated they were from a nearby police barracks, were sparring—practicing strikes, kicks, and takedowns. He recognized many techniques, but never had he seen them executed with such economy, speed, and power. They drew from many arts, such as aikido and jiu-jitsu, but he soon realized that its integration of them, along with many subtle refinements, was uniquely powerful.

For an hour, he sat on the beach and watched. "Remember," the instructor called out, "your top priority must always be to identify when you need to kill or else be killed yourself. Or, short of killing, you need to be able immediately to assess the possible outcome and intensity of various dangers, and instantaneously respond. For this you must stay aware of your breath. Breathing is the bridge between mind and body."

For every skill, timing was the key principle. "You must always execute both defense and attack at the same time," the instructor stressed. "Any pause, can mean your life." For Armando, all this distilled to essentials what he had learned over the years—not for sport competitions—but for real-world, life-and-death situations. He sensed, even then, that one day he would use—*need*—such skills.

The instructor was an old man with a slight frame encased in hardened sinew. Armando found that he had been an Israeli commando with a lifetime of experience in special operations. The man was impressed with the boy's skills and was attracted by his intense sincerity. Armando spent a year traveling the Caribbean, training with him one-on-one, including underwater fighting, and, in exchange, assisting him when he taught classes. And that was frequently, for he was very much in demand. For Armando, it was his most formative year of martial training.

Armando's first love, however, was actually another category of arts, the visual: Painting, sculpting, interior design, and landscape design. His greatest emotional rush in life was to bring something new into existence, something unique, which had never been seen before.

He worked in many media, until settling on watercolor as his favorite. Marek Rankl was exploring a remote Caribbean beach, an activity he indulged whenever he could make the time. He came across a man creating a watercolor painting. He was sitting in the sand, wearing shorts, unbuttoned shirt, and a wide straw hat. His feet were bare, and a large watercolor block was propped in front of him. Near it were pigments, brushes, mixing trays, and a water bottle. The lettering on his wooden supply case read *Armando Rojas*.

As Marek approached, he could see a vivid watercolor taking shape. A red bandana was around the artist's neck, and every several seconds his head looked out to the scene before him. Marek was captivated by what he saw feverishly taking shape on the watercolor sheet. But he said nothing. He backed well away and stayed away, even as the man dozed, to give the paper time to dry before taking up his brushes again. Finally, Marek knew he was done.

When he reached the artist, he found him totally absorbed, *contemplating* what he had wrought. He had eyes for nothing else. Marek squatted next to him, saying nothing. He stared for long moments. The brilliant translucence of the sky, the energy in the ocean water, and the intricacy of the washes, was the backdrop for a riot of gulls swooping and shrieking in wild abandon over the waves, as they fed on a school of silver wrasses. Marek was mesmerized. Finally, he simply said to the artist, "There must be no feeling like it, to have done something like this."

It was only then that the man looked at Marek. He sensed that this stranger was speaking from experience, though of a different kind. Marek saw a face older than his own. "It is the meaning of life, this feeling," the man replied, turning his head back to it. "Yes, it is," Marek replied. The artist turned back to Marek again. There had been quiet reverence in this stranger's voice; a bond had been established.

That evening, Armando Rojas and his guest surf-fished for bonitos and then grilled them on a patio overlooking the beach. Celia Rojas's great success with her music, and Armando's with his paintings, made possible simple seaside homes on a number of Caribbean islands. This island was one of them.

The two men discovered that, although they were totally different in background, they were completely alike in what they held most precious in life—the joy of bringing something new into existence—the joy of *creating*.

Celia's concert career was long over, but she serenaded them that evening, her virtuosity on the guitar still evident. Armando had learned guitar from her when he was very young and had played all his life. He and his mother did a duet that evening—one of her famous compositions—and Marek saw another side of his new friend.

Alek and Marek still stood in front of Armando's watercolor—his painting of that fateful meeting of Marek and Besosa, the better part of 100 years ago. Then Alek saw his great-grandfather's face return to the present, and they had breakfast.

Alek asked him about longevity and age reversal. But Marek only smiled and said, "All in good time, my son. He then abruptly changed the subject, informing Alek that, after the remaining three portals, he would be ready to tour Arête. The tour might take a number of days, he said, but he assured Alek it would fill in a lot of the blanks, including age-reversal research on Arête.

He also told him, "Liang has insisted on being your guide," and he saw his great-grandson's face break into a smile.

DRAGON & HELIX

It was Alek's fifth day on Oribel, and he was about to enter the next portal, *Defense*, when he heard the soft hum of an air vehicle. He looked up and saw that it was Marek's, its wings waving, before it flew off in the direction of Arête.

Initiating the portal, he once again found himself on the top floor of Vindauge Tower in Manhattan, two thousand miles north of Oribel. He walked into the conference room and, as before, was drawn to a seat which put him directly across from the lectern on the opposite side of the huge, square table. He saw Lenore, Armando, and a sandy-haired man whom he did not recognize, standing in conversation with Marek, near the lectern. They took their seats, and Marek started.

"Yesterday," he said, "we covered human capital, government, constitution, and the Foundation. Today we will cover a final major priority, defense. As Art Haag pointed out, the Frontier Foundation, years earlier, had chartered various teams to further develop RME's already-extensive defense system and to do so with the Prometheus Frontier in mind.

"Defense of the Frontier has shaped up to be even more challenging and complex than we had originally thought. I know you are already aware of that. Over the years we often had occasion to discuss it, in company meetings as well as in one-on-one conversations. Today and tomorrow, we will bring it all together, and here is our program." He looked up to the hologram.

DEFENSE

The Great Conflict
Hard Defense
Soft Defense
Flamekeepers
Recapitulation

"I will start with the first item, the Great Conflict. This will set the overall context for why defense is so vital to the survival of the Frontier. Jerrold Makara, who heads our hard defense system, will have that item, followed by Lenore Pellon with soft defense. Finally, Armando Rojas will introduce his brain child, the Flamekeepers. So, once again, let us begin.

"Regarding overall context, I want you to consider the Prometheus Frontier and our vision. Consider what we are doing. *Really* consider it. We are creating an island nation which absolutely banishes the initiation of physical force. We are banishing not only its *physical* expression but, vastly more important, we are banishing the *threat* of physical force—its most common expression.

"Observe the world around you; scan the pages of human history. Look into your souls, where past experiences of such threats are etched. In any social system that does not absolutely banish the initiation of force against another, there exists a single great reality. That reality is the *threat* that initiated physical force can happen at any time. *This*, I submit, is an even greater evil than *actual* physical force, for this threat is a constant looming, corrosive presence in the soul.

"The Prometheus Frontier is creating a different reality. We are forming a social system of profound peace. Yet it is also a social system whose survival will be profoundly at risk from two inescapable facts of human nature.

"First is the fact of volition. We are volitional beings, capable of choosing good or evil. There will always be *some* individuals who choose the latter, such as those who seek to achieve their values through physical force against others, rather than through voluntary production and trade.

"The second fact of human nature is envy. Many people—not all, but many—feel envy when they see another's good fortune and resent the fact that it is not their own. Envy will often—not always, but often—lead people forcibly to seek to take possession of the good fortune of others—*steal* it. Envy can be a very ugly emotion.

"Unfortunately, the Prometheus Frontier is establishing a society that will, inadvertently evoke this emotion and the physical force to which it often leads. Throughout history, envious resentment has led people, societies, even whole nations to expropriate the good fortune of others, that is, take possession of it by physical force.

"This is the source of the vital need for a powerful defense system. Without it, the Prometheus Frontier, with its unimaginably prosperous social system, would positively invite annihilation. It would be a mere matter of time.

The great conflict is between those who produce and those who take from the producer, from those who trade and those who steal.

"The lesson to us from history is crystal clear: Defend thyself or be destroyed."

Dragon & Helix

When Jerrold Makara got up to present hard defense, Alek recognized the sandy-haired man who had been with Lenore and Armando before Marek started his opening remarks. Makara commenced by indicating he was a cyber scientist by trade, one of a sizeable cadre of RME scientists of various disciplines. Alek watched and listened intently.

"As you know," Makara said, "our hard defense system started life some years ago, with a charter from the Frontier Foundation. The charter was challenging: Create a defense system possessing two essential characteristics—lethality and impregnability—and do so through an unmatched control of cyberspace.

"Rankl Marine Enterprises, from its inception, has always experienced cyberattack as the greatest threat from the world at large. Often it would be in the form of cyber espionage, and often it would be in the form of outright cyber assault. Of necessity, RME has had to become very savvy in the control of cyberspace, in all its aspects.

Now keep that in mind, as I lay out for you, in broad outline, our weapons for countering cyberattack." He looked up to the hologram.

HARD DEFENSE

DRAGON
Deadly Repelling of AGgressiON

HELIX
Dragon's Technology

Dragon, as you can see, is an acronym for Deadly Repelling of Aggression.

"Dragon repels cyberattacks, whether planned or actual. In the case of an *actual* attack, it takes control of the weapon's programming, and reverses the attack *against* the attacker.

"But this is not Dragon's primary mode of operation. Its primary mode addresses *planned* cyberattacks. Most Frontier actions, to date, have been preemptive and *not* generally public. Preemptive actions repel *planned* attacks *before* they occur by taking control of the computer systems on which they depend. Once it has control, it renders the attack weapon unusable, and destroys it, or turns it against the plotter, and *then* destroys it.

"The Frontier's intelligence arm is what makes preemption possible. We are in possession of the most comprehensive and intensive intelligence system the human mind has ever created, and *this*, by an exponential margin. When we get to Helix, the second item on our agenda, you'll understand why I can make this claim.

"Finally, attacks actual and planned aside, dragon also has the capability of bringing down basic infrastructures of enemy nations or entities—by destroying the computer systems on which their infrastructures depend. RME's hard defense system has long had this capability but has yet to deploy it.

"But the Frontier could very well *need* to deploy this weapon system when confronted with an especially egregious attack, an unspeakable atrocity, for instance. In such a case, the capability of which we speak needs to be deployed. And when such a need arises, deployment will surely occur, to punish, to preclude recurrence, and to deter even the *thought* of anything like it recurring."

Makara called for a break, and the buffet table briefly became the room's center of attention. Alek once again found he had been served a container of coffee and something to eat. From his seat, he several times heard questions regarding the decision-making process behind Dragon.

"Let's take a few minutes and talk about decision making," Makara said upon resuming. "A number of you asked me about it during the break. For now, however, I'll simply indicate that it is the Frontier Foundation which holds war powers authority. But details are not final yet. Who and how many in the Foundation will hold these powers? For what types of attacks or threats do they hold them? How are these powers balanced? Eventually, such issues will be encoded in the Frontier's constitution, draft forms of which, will be reviewed by all in this room. But for now, it's still work in process.

"You also need to remember," Makara continued, "that, as you learned a little while ago, most deployment of Dragon will be preemptive and based on comprehensive intelligence. Of course, once again, the Frontier's constitution needs to define who in the Foundation holds decision power and for what *type* of action. In any case, when the mode of operation is preemption, there would be time for measured consideration before deployment.

"In the case of imminent threat, of course, it's a different story," Makara went on. "You can be sure, that a delayed response will *not* be an option. Again, the constitution will define circumstances and contingencies, to the extent possible."

Makara asked if there were further questions, but there were none. "The second major element of hard defense is Helix," he resumed. "Helix is not an acronym, but rather, a term which captures the element's essential microbial nature.

"Helix grew out of DNA Nanoscience, a field that actually began life quite some time ago. This new field led to many initiatives around the world to develop supercomputers whose microprocessors were made of DNA rather than silicon chips. DNA—Deoxyribonucleic Acid—is a living molecule and, like all living entities, self-replicates. This gave DNA supercomputers the magic-like power of *growing* as they compute. No longer was a computer limited to a fixed number of microprocessors, and this led to a revolutionary, orders-of-magnitude advance in miniaturization, memory capacity, and problem-solving ability.

"Everyone in this room knows well that, over the years, RME's Foundation committed enormous resources toward developing DNA supercomputing. And, indeed, the return on investment has been exponential. DNA supercomputing has been the building block of RME's phenomenal success.

"DNA supercomputing has also been the building block of RME's defense and intelligence systems. Consequently, defense of the Prometheus Frontier, for the first time, has approached impregnability. And none of this would have happened without RME's revolutionary development and exploitation of DNA supercomputing. That is a certainty.

"Helix is a distributed computer system with no central program or database. A team of cyber scientists and programmers administer it, but there is no one person who holds all the spirals and strands together. Additionally, because all elements of Helix have multiple redundancies, there is no failure mode that would bring it down."

A voice called out, "That's quite a claim, attended by a wealth of technical detail. But explain how it is hack proofed." Everyone knew it was Marek Rankl playing the devil's advocate, looking to stir things up a bit. The presentation had become intensely technical.

Makara did not miss a beat. "The explanation actually is less technical," he replied with a smile, "at least in its name. The

Frontier's weapon systems are protected by *crumb detector* technology, unique to us. Everyone in the world has its way of searching out crumbs, the residue of enemy activity. But our crumb detector technology proceeds from an exponentially advanced application of DNA supercomputing. No one comes close, and that will not change, for we are continually improving and refining it.

"Enter one Lenore Pellon, philosopher," Makara concluded. "Lenore is next on our agenda and will present soft defense. She brings another perspective to the Prometheus Frontier's defense strategy. Her fresh perspective has augmented all that we had already been doing. *Most* importantly, however, Lenore has significantly impacted our thinking—and priorities."

Alek looked forward to Lenore with intense interest. I wonder whether she felt the same concern I'm feeling, he thought to himself, the feeling that Jerrold Makara was being a bit overconfident?

Galea Magre and a trusted aide exited Pangaia Island's International Assembly Hall into the long corridor that would take them back to her office. The aide was her main sounding board before and after each main presentation, and they were discussing this afternoon's. It had been her crisis address regarding the existence of Arête and why it had reached the level of a crisis and had to be stopped.

As they passed a dim alcove, she heard a dry whisper-like voice come up from the bench within the recess. "Madam Secretary, a moment of your time, if you please." The voice froze her. She immediately recognized the chilling, sinister quality of it. It was a voice from her past. She dismissed her aide and turned to face the darkness from which the voice had come.

During her graduate school years in New York City, Galea Magre had belonged to a revolutionary band of Marxist intellectuals. It was comprised of many nationalities, united by a common purpose. All were young, idealistic, and consumed by totalitarian ideologies. They were also united by something further. Each was disillusioned by the usual strategies employed to replace free enterprise with central authority: culture cancellation, career destruction, and above all, mind control through an iron-like grip on education, private conscience, and the internet.

The disillusioned members chafed at the long-term nature of such strategies. A small core broke off to form a cadre specializing in an alternative approach: asymmetric warfare. This approach used deception and unpredictability to defeat an enemy no matter how otherwise impenetrable its defenses might be. Success depended on one all-important element: intense planning, underpinned by an all-embracing loyalty and secrecy. This element was the cadre's strength.

Galea Magre had known its leader intimately, both intellectually and physically. Hers was the whisper-like voice she had just heard for the first time in many years. The woman behind the voice had been virtually present at Magre's address today, from one of the many media stations in the building. She was determined that it was Galea Magre's turn to listen to her. Her name was Gina Pudaro, and she was confident that Magre was ready. Listening to today's address to the international assembly, she had detected great frustration.

The two women faced each other in Magre's condominium apartment that evening. They had been talking for the past two hours, and they were close to concluding.

Magre noticed that her guest had not changed much over the decades. Gina Pudaro still wore her hair cropped short and dressed severely. Her black suit was impeccably tailored, nicely set off by violet suede pumps whose color was picked up by a plain blouse of the same color.

This was a dramatic style upgrade from the young revolutionary, Magre thought to herself. But the voice was the same dry whispery one resulting from years of heavy smoking. That voice was now summarizing her case before Forthright magazine's most influential woman in the world.

"So, you see Madame Secretary, we can never win the intellectual battle—the battle our common enemy is so practiced in. Our enemy, that island 2000 miles south of where we sit at this moment is, from its very founding, and in its every argument, based on reason, a faculty that uses logical argument to make its every case. Declaration of Freedom indeed!" Pudaro's voice hissed. "The declaration is a tissue of rationalization, not reason. It makes arguments that *pretend* to be rational but are no more than excuses, rationalizations, to justify the ongoing exploitation of the working classes. Reason is not the way to deal with such an enemy. Physical force is—specifically asymmetric force."

Magre reached for the wine bottle and pored. Pudaro waited, confident that they were already in agreement. She watched her host take a sip and silently sit, mulling it all over.

Finally, Magre spoke. "So, let's summarize. The scientists in your stable have an absolutely foolproof method of getting this to happen?"

"Absolutely."

"What evidence do you have?"

"We have dealt with these scientists many times over the years, in many parts of the world. They have been behind every successful asymmetric attack for the past half century. They have proven themselves time and again."

"What's to keep the Frontier's defense system from detecting it in advance and stopping it? It has an uncanny ability to detect and take preemptive action, before any attack is even launched. It has proved it can do this."

"I answer your question in one word: Asymmetry. The diabolical attack I have laid out for you is essentially based on two features: deception and unpredictability. The Frontier's defenses do not have the means of dealing with asymmetric warfare."

"Diabolical is an understatement. I never in my life imagined a weapon so horrendous."

"This is not a time to be squeamish. Harsh times require harsh solutions. And sometimes complete annihilation is the *only* solution. The Prometheus Frontier is one such cause. It has to be gone."

"Explain again how we deflect suspicion away from Pangaia, in the aftermath."

"Once the attack is public, you do that by proclaiming Pangaia's willingness to help in any way that you can. This is all part of the deception element of asymmetric warfare. We will talk more about this as the deadline draws closer. For now, this is all you need to know. Of course, you know, and I know, that the island would never take you up on such an offer. Still, simply the fact that you made it, will carry weight in the court of world opinion."

Magre's body language indicated she was finally satisfied. Gina Pudaro stopped talking, and Magre knew her guest was on an encrypted telebot call, with a device somewhere on her person. She mentally ordered her own bot's mind-read function to engage. And unbeknownst to Pudaro, her side of the telepathic exchange was absorbed by her host.

Yes, I'll be leaving shortly. Pick me up across the avenue from her main entrance. Yes, she knows that it's fail safe, but she had to be convinced. That's why we were so long this evening. Fear not, we have a go.

―――

WARRIORS OF THE MIND

It was another day for Alek Rankl in New York City's Vindauge Tower. Yesterday, the concentration had been hard defense; today would focus on intellectual, or soft defense.

When the eleventh portal, *Warriors of the Mind*, transported him to the tower's eightieth floor conference room, Alek once again found himself in a seat opposite the lectern on the other side of the room. Above, the hologram displayed the day's agenda.

SOFT DEFENSE

Basic Premises
Elements
Defense Recap
Flamekeepers

Then, as Alek arrived, Lenore greeted the room, paused, and began. "First, I want to say a few words about today's agenda. The first three items deal with soft defense. When I've finished, Marek will do a brief overall recap of the Frontier's hard and soft defense systems. After that, Armando Rojas will entertain us with the final agenda item, Flamekeepers.

"So, with that, let's start by defining exactly what we mean by soft defense? Quite simply, the Frontier's soft defense consists of intellectual weapons designed to counter the hostile attacks of enemy propaganda. Such attacks are biased, misleading, and all too often, blatantly false. Yesterday, Marek clearly spelled out the unavoidable reality of such attacks due to the fact that, among others, resentment is a human emotion, all too real in many people, when they see that others are more prosperous than they are. This resentment gets expressed in many ways through enemy propaganda—propaganda which commonly leads to physical violence. Sometimes propaganda deliberately *incites* physical violence.

"For the Frontier, the major source of enemy propaganda is the organization we know as Pangaia. This is the organization to which all the world's nations pledge allegiance. And it means that they also pledge fealty to the social philosophy of Herbert Henry, its founder. Henry's doctrines are a blend of classical Marxism, its twentieth and twenty-first century spinoffs, and religious authoritarianism. This toxic mix is diametrically opposed to everything for which the Prometheus Frontier stands. And what is most important for us to realize, it fuels Pangaia's propaganda machine.

"Media outlets around the globe follow suit and reflect the Herbert Henry playscript. The intensity of all this spewed hatred will surely be ramping up with the inauguration of Arête as the first island nation of the Prometheus Frontier. It is imperative, therefore, that such propaganda be countered—and this is where soft defense comes in.

"The Prometheus Frontier's soft defense system deploys three intellectual weapons to counter enemy propaganda. Weapon one is formidable intellectual power. As you know, the frontier is already a magnet for the world's best brains, many of whom dedicate themselves to soft defense. Of course, internally, Arête's superlative educational system supports that cadre. And that brings us to weapon two.

"Weapon two is a mobilized citizenry—an *intellectually* mobilized citizenry. It starts in our schools with the study of history, and later with the study of philosophy. This latter is a tricky area, for it requires a certain amount of life experience. But we find that youthful Arêteans seek out philosophy courses because, inadvertently, we have endowed those courses with a certain aura. This happens whenever courses—ours are examples—are offered as electives for the mature, advanced student, and similar wording. As a result, we have a population of young adults with an unusual exposure to philosophy. Please hold that thought; I'll have more to say about the importance of philosophy in a few minutes, when I talk about defense infrastructure.

"Weapon three is aggressive intellectual activism. This activism continually publicizes to the world that the Frontier is a profound force for good. We must always keep that message out there. The Prometheus Frontier upholds human life as the ultimate value, and holds, as its number one mission—its number one *moral* mission—the advancement of human flourishing."

Lenore paused to sip from a water bottle, and asked how everyone was doing with this, so far. Karen McTeague again spoke up and, this time, commented that aggressive intellectual activism sounded like preemptive strikes in the arena of hard defense—removing threats before they can wreak their havoc. "Exactly right," Lenore replied. "The old saw, that the best defense is a good offense, applies to soft defense, as surely as it does to hard defense. Just as with hard defense, the soft defense system must anticipate threats, detect them before they surface, and then neutralize them. Essentially, hard and soft defense are the same in that respect.

"And they are also equally necessary; if anything, intellectual activism in the soft weapon arena is even more necessary than preemptive strikes in the hard weapon arena. The main reason for saying this is because the long-term survival of the Frontier depends on aggressive intellectual activism to foster allies throughout the world. It is a very, very big world out there, and we will not survive without allies.

"Now let's take still another perspective on soft defense," Lenore continued. "Let's talk infrastructure—*philosophic* infrastructure. The social system of the Frontier is underpinned by a culture imbued with a reverence for human life, for the mind, for thinking. The greatest evidence of this is that we have banished the initiation of physical force or any threat of it as the greatest of social evils. Our conviction is absolute that retaliatory force against such evil is a moral necessity—*and our sacred right*. All of this is *philosophy*. And let us not forget the Frontier's Declaration of Freedom. Above all else, our Declaration of Freedom is advancing a philosophy. All these are essential elements of the potent philosophic infrastructure which underpins our soft defense system. Indeed, it is the infrastructure which underpins the Frontier's entire culture."

After a short break Marek was back at the lectern. "Before I introduce Armando, I want briefly to recap four vitally important points regarding the Prometheus Frontier's defense system.

"Point one is that we have defined our defense system to be impregnable, or as close to that as possible. We take as axiomatic the reality that, without an impervious defense system, any island of freedom in the world will surely lose that freedom to dictatorial power. Without impervious defense, it would be a mere matter of time.

"Point two is that our defense system includes two types of weapons: hard—*physical* weapons, and soft—*intellectual* weapons. And, of the two, intellectual weapons are more vital. Without intellectual weapons, hard weapons are of limited value, and, inevitably, without teeth. That is, without intellectual weapons, which provide the will to deploy them, hard weapons are reduced to the stuff of paper tigers.

"Even in our century, mere decades ago, island states favorable to freedom in the South China Sea were forcibly taken over; one by one, they were swallowed up by a dictatorial power. Neither they, nor their powerful allies in the world, had the necessary intellectual weapons to deter or stop it. I am talking about the weapons that would have given them the courage to deploy, or seriously *threaten* to deploy their formidable hard weapons. Thus, do dictatorial powers go undeterred and unpunished, and islands of freedom get lost. History is witness to how common this has been—and how recent.

"Point three is the Frontier's willingness to deploy its hard defense system unilaterally. This is already built into our Declaration of Freedom. There is no higher authority that we would recognize—certainly not any international body. As our declaration makes clear, the only authority we recognize is human reason, and we must always start with our own.

"Point four is the Frontier's rejection of multiculturalism. The idea that we must respect all cultures and grant all of them equal moral status—multiculturalism—is, in essence, itself immoral. Any culture that fails to respect individual rights is, by that fact alone, less than moral. Any such culture is a rogue culture, and any state sanctioning such a culture is a rogue state. It has forfeited any claim to moral stature. Those are the four points I wanted to make," he concluded.

Warriors of the Mind

Alek saw Marek pause and look up to the hologram. The word *Flamekeepers* had appeared. "We now come to one of my favorite subjects, the Flamekeepers," he started. "Flamekeepers is a term originated by Armando Rojas.

"Armando and I first met nearly twenty years ago on a remote Caribbean beach where he was creating one of his luminous watercolors. It was the start of a great friendship. We soon discovered that we shared the same view of what is most sacred in life. All of you are familiar with Armando the artist: his watercolor paintings and his sculptures.

"And, of course, we all know Armando Rojas as another kind of artist—a superbly accomplished *martial* artist. Those of you who have trained in any of the martial arts know that such skills require the development of a finely tuned integration of mind and body. Armando possesses this quality to an extraordinary degree. It was only natural, as we were developing the Frontier's defenses—Armando was involved from the outset—that he would have insights that the ordinary person was less likely to have. Armando, if you please," he said as he gestured toward his friend.

A tall man, in loose-fitting exercise garb and bronzed by a lifetime in the Caribbean sun, sprung from his seat and took the lectern. For the second time since the chartering of Paine a few days ago, the room suddenly filled with applause. Armando greeted them with a familiar martial salute, bringing his two hands together in front of him, right fist to left palm, and inclining his head forward slightly while continuing to hold their gaze.

There was a magnetic aura to the man. His deep-set eyes were intense, and his straight mouth was outlined by neatly trimmed hair under his nose, continuing down under his jaw. His cleft chin and gaunt cheeks were bare and contrasted with a full head of wavy, graying hair.

"I want to start with some footage," he said, as the hologram went to the sizeable martial arts facility two floors below the one they were on. Over the next several minutes, Armando, Marek, and Lenore—sweatbands on their foreheads, and workout gear on their bodies—gave a demonstration, uniquely choreographed by their trainer for the four-sided hologram. It started with a set of basic self-defense moves and then proceeded to a remarkable display of ever more complex techniques. Armando loved demonstrating how simply grabbing a pinky and twisting the right way can easily bring an aggressor's face down to the ground, at which point he was at the mercy of the erstwhile victim. Lenore had the honor of demonstrating that technique—on *him*, to the delight of all in the room.

The show went on from that point, gradually increasing in tempo and complexity. By the end, Armando, Marek, and Lenore were going through a furious display of rapid-fire moves, grapples, take-downs, and pins. They took turns as attacker and defender. Every attack was met with a lightning-like strike or kick or grab to a readily accessible pressure point. It could be kneecap, groin, or carotid. Or it could be eyes, nose, or windpipe. Whatever its target—the counterattack stopped just short of contact or completion—so fast that it was not really perceived until it had actually reached that stopping point. "The objective," Armando's voice said from the lectern, "is always to defend and counterattack in one motion. Any hesitation can be the difference between life and death."

Finally, the vid went into loop mode. Armando kept it running but lowered the volume. Applause briefly filled the room once again. "What you see is an eclectic hybrid of styles and techniques from the vast and fascinating world of martial arts," he pointed out. "But despite the diversity of the techniques you see, each style shares—actually *requires*—one common quality. Each of them demands a complete integration of mind and body.

One cannot excel without that integration. And not to excel is to flirt with grave danger.

"Arête's Flamekeeper program is built on the same model: mind-body integration. I've witnessed the evolution of the Prometheus Frontier for a number of years now and, early on, I identified a vulnerability—a very significant vulnerability. Consider this. Arête, as Marek and Lenore have stated, will have a social system of profound peace. Now ask yourself what will keep Arêteans from becoming soft as time goes on. Oh sure, they can be kept fired up by the infrastructure Lenore pointed to. No question about that. But that's in their head. Is that enough for physical commitment, when physical action is needed? The ancient Spartans didn't think so and neither do I.

"Not that Arête needs to recreate Sparta. That was far more extreme than what we need, and worse, it had definite unhealthy elements. I'm not going to go into them here. Instead, I want you to be aware that training in the martial arts, properly executed, is unsurpassed in its ability to build confidence, character, and self-discipline. But it goes far beyond these necessary and wonderful qualities. One of my masters used to put it like this. He used to say that those of us who have studied and trained in the martial disciplines experience a great security and calm in life. It is the security and calm one needs to excel in any other field and truly to walk in peace. The essence of this at the individual level is the integration of mind and body.

"Let me be quite definite about this. There is no other discipline, anywhere, in any field, that accomplishes what Martial Arts training does, when properly taught. For exercise, physical fitness, camaraderie, and sheer fun, martial arts training has it all. But above all else in importance, is *mental fitness*—self-confidence and self-worth—martial arts training has no equal.

"As children, whether boy or girl, if we had enlightened parents, they exposed us to basic self-defense training; this was a great gift. With basic self-defense training, suddenly, children can handle themselves in the face of a bully. Suddenly, the child has the self-confidence to face a physical threat. The child, for the first time, has become armed spiritually—*intellectually*. If the training emphasizes it, as all good training must, the child has an integrated body and mind and can, for the first time in life, walk in peace, ready to face an adversary when appropriate or, without shame, simply walk away when *that* is appropriate.

"Note that children don't need the advanced skills you saw Marek, Lenore, and I demonstrating. But those advanced skills are there to learn, for those who want them. Many will pursue them simply as part of the quest to be ever improving, another emphasis of martial arts training.

"For some Arêteans, advanced training is actually required. The martial arts program I have designed for Arête has many unique features and can be tailored in any number of ways. But for Arête's special forces—yes, it is essential we have special forces—advanced skills such as you saw us demonstrating—are indispensable. Additionally, there are the skills with knives and firearms, skills needed in water combat, and arcane ninjutsu weapons and techniques, which have application in certain situations.

Regardless of skills sought, and regardless of motivation, my program is totally comprehensive and adaptable to anyone's needs or interests. Special forces, of course, is of necessity a very select group. For most Arêtean youth, martial arts are simply there for self-improvement and self-discipline. They are completely voluntary. But they are so public, so well publicized, and clearly so much fun, that few are the Arêteans who do not pursue martial training at some time. And, whatever the level, few are the Arêtean youth, who do not incorporate it into their lifestyle.

Warriors of the Mind

"As to the need for special forces, consider that, despite aggressive soft defense, and seemingly impregnable hard defense, Arête is still open to water attack, or terror attack, or infiltration by those seeking to become hidden, internal enemies. And these are just for starters. Bottom line: Arête is a small island nation, exposed to a hostile world. We have vulnerabilities; make no mistake about it.

"That brings us to the arena of *special-ops*—boots-on-ground or, for an island nation, fins-in-sea operations. These would be needed for both retaliatory and preemptive actions, as well as other missions. Consider the need to liaison with freedom fighters elsewhere in the world, the need to cultivate them as allies, and to assist them in their endeavors, if only through moral support. The Frontier's special-force flamekeepers would be ideally suited for all such missions. And they would have the respect of all with whom they come into contact. They would have had the necessary training to command that respect.

"Flamekeepers will always be needed if the Prometheus Frontier is to survive and flourish long term," Armando declared, as he approached the end of his presentation. "It is a way of mobilizing Arêteans, young and old, always to be on a war footing while at the same time living in peace and flourishing.

"There are many features we still need to work out. But work them out, we will. And the result will be a defense system whose elements, hard and soft, are all the more fully integrated, and thereby enhanced. It will be a defense system whose body and mind are one, and whose population is one—everyone ever vigilant to preserve and protect the survival and flourishing of the Prometheus Frontier."

———

INAUGURATION

Alek found himself back in Ventana Garden on the island of Oribel. He was still standing before the portal from which he had just returned, the eleventh. It had been another full day.

When Marek welcomed him in portal one, he had called this garden of portals a gauntlet, of sorts. Alek now understood why. The sheer volume of what he had needed to absorb and digest was staggering. It felt like five years of time had passed since he started when, in fact, it had been a mere five days.

He thought of the people he had met, both in real time, and in the virtual time of the portals. In the case of Marek, it had been both. He thought of the arc of his great-grandfather's life: childhood, formative years studying microbiology and philosophy, Ocean Polytechnic Institute, Rankl Marine Enterprises and great fortune. Lenore Pellon, the greatest of all fortunes.

Alek knew that all this, and so much more, had been a preamble to the momentous event that he was now poised to witness; it was announced on the final portal plate, several feet from where he stood: *Inauguration*. But that would be tomorrow.

Before exiting onto the path back to the island's small mountain, he walked the garden. He was thinking of all he had learned about the Frontier's defenses. What was Marek's involvement in defense now, he wondered, then realized that he had surely left it in the hands of his scientists and business directors, along with a vast army of managers and engineers. The lure of the next *new* venture, Alek knew, would always be beckoning a mind like his great-grandfather's.

He approached the air vehicle landing pad, but instead of continuing on to the lift, he turned and walked toward the pier. He looked out to the water and pondered the Frontier's defenses. As he stood there, he recalled Davesh Navendra saying that he wanted to tap his brain. Alek recalled his years of work on the great problem of cyber defense: Impregnability. Any nation could become the target of a deadly attack on its most important infrastructure: the computer and satellite systems controlling everything else. A nation, so attacked, would be at the mercy of the attacker; total annihilation could be the result.

After Jerrold Makara's presentation yesterday, he realized that he had contributions to make. Davesh Navendra had sensed it the day they met, when Alek had alluded to impregnability via an algorithm on which he had been working for a number of years. Suddenly, he had a burning desire—*need*—to share his thinking with Navendra. He turned and headed back to the lift. He had seen the scientist's AV in the landing area several minutes ago; it meant he was in the Neuron Center.

Alek and Davesh talked late into the evening. Each man had much to share with the other, as well as learn *from* the other. Davesh probed deeply, as did Alek. The bond between them continued to grow.

Alek explained his hypothesis that for a cyber defense system to reach the holy grail of impregnability, two necessary conditions had to be met. The system had to be sensitive to unpredictability for one, and to deception for the other. Throughout the history of warfare, these two strategies, unpredictability and deception, were great power amplifiers of any weapon system. Conversely, their absence explained the failure of many a great power in history.

For a number of years, Alek had been working to integrate unpredictability and deception into an algorithm which, running in the background of a cyber defense system, would make it all but impregnable. Without this algorithm, serious vulnerabilities would always exist; they were inherent in the very nature of cyberspace.

Navendra explored Alek's algorithm in depth. Together they dug into the complexities behind each element, and then their integration. Alek explained the causal factors involved and the underlying mathematics enabling their integration.

Davesh examined the programming code and noted Alek's unique method of hyper-encryption. As Alek conveyed to the scientist his still-evolving thoughts on the quest for system-wide impregnability, Navendra saw enormous potential. He was thrilled by the way Alek's mind worked.

Alek was astounded by the sophistication of Neuron, a sophistication going far beyond the surface appearances of the center. Eighty-five years had transpired from the time of Makara's presentation on *Dragon* and *Helix*, virtually attended by Alek in the portal. Now, as Davesh conveyed the Neuron Center's subsequent evolution, further ideas flooded Alek's mind. He realized that their holy grail would actually be a perpetual quest in the face of continuously evolving challenges.

But he also knew that he could think of no better way to use his mind—no more *exciting* way. There would be no end to the need to keep growing, starting with fully grasping the deeply microbial nature of everything happening in Neuron. For Alek, to be continuously growing was one of life's great joys, as he suspected was also the case for Davesh. Indeed, each of them was realizing that it was the root of the bond they felt.

Inauguration

Liang had arrived from Arête with a simple evening meal. They ate in Neuron's small cafeteria, with Rhee and Eric joining them. It seemed a long time to Alek since he had seen Liang, and he could tell, from the way she greeted him, that she felt the same way.

That night, Alek collapsed onto a spare bed in Neuron. As he fell asleep, he thought of the last thing Davesh had said before they stopped for the evening. "Yes, you really have identified a vulnerability," Davesh Navendra had said. "I don't think it is too late, but I can't help wishing you had gotten here sooner." When Alek awoke, he found himself covered with an extra blanket. Navendra himself rarely slept more than three hours a night.

The next morning, when Alek arrived in the long room, he found his aunt and uncle still at breakfast with Marek. He heard Liang's air vehicle hovering outside; then she waved goodbye and banked for Arête. She had spent the night in her bedroom in the cliff dwelling.

"We talked with Davesh this morning," Marek told him. "We can't remember ever seeing him so excited."

"I'm excited too," Alek replied. "You know, although Dragon and Helix were amazing eighty-five years ago—and I realize they remain foundational—they could not even start to prepare me for the realms Davesh took me into last night."

"One more portal, and you'll be ready for your Arête tour," Eric said.

"And Liang is still insisting that she shepherd you," Rhee smiled.

"Today's portal is the final one," Marek told him. "Over the years, many others have been through all twelve portals. As you

Inauguration

know from Eric and Rhee, the holo-lasic portal is the vehicle by which we preserve the vital history of the Prometheus Frontier.

"You have become a key member of the team chartered to ensure that the Frontier never goes out of existence. But still, it remains conceivable that that could happen. There is no guarantee that it will not. And if it did, the portals capture the key elements that would be needed to guide rebuilding, not least of which are the vision and the inspiration. Over the years, we have often been told by graduates of the portal program that number twelve, *Inauguration*, is the most inspiring portal of them all.

"This is as it should be," Marek concluded. "The inauguration was the culmination of a great struggle to begin the world over again, on Arête, and the start of an ongoing struggle to survive and flourish in a world that would seek to end it."

When Alek initiated the *Inauguration* portal, the holo-lasic data stream filling the ambient air space before him included the faint drone of hydrogen engines. He found himself in an air vehicle above the Caribbean, heading for Arête Island on the horizon, ten miles distant.

A soft female voice announced that seventy-five years ago, the island nation of Arête officially celebrated its birth—a momentous one, marking for the first time in history, the beginning of a nation explicitly banishing the initiation of physical force from all human affairs, public as well as private. "Today," the voice continued, "you will witness the climax of that historical event, the lighting of the perpetual flame in Arête's harbor. It happened here, at the rock structure you are now approaching."

Inauguration

The air vehicle slowed as it drew closer. Alek looked down to the unlit torch rising above the rocks rising seventy-five feet out of the ocean. Upon ignition, the flame would burst upward from it. Waves crashed against the rocks below, and the gulls perching on them stood out in white relief.

The AV continued toward Aréte, the soft hum of its engines the only sound. As it brought Alek closer, the sea wall and esplanade of an earlier Aréte came into view. Looking to the island's eastern tip, he could see the Arétean flag, its golden flame luminous in the morning sun, snapping in the breeze, above an acoustic shell.

The shell embraced a concert stage facing a large commons which was gradually filling with Arêteans. They were on benches lining the paths of the commons. Others were on chairs they had brought with them. Many others were relaxing on the ground, on colorful beach towels. Families with children were on blankets. There were also groups, here and there, standing in conversation.

The air vehicle gradually dropped in altitude, slowly bringing the stage into focus, below the acoustic shell. A man at the podium faced the audience in the commons, and the vidstream panned the faces of the two dozen men and women sitting behind him on the stage. The soft voice resumed, "Of course, you recognize Marek at the podium; the other figures are founding members of the Paine Society, some of whom you'll recognize as well."

The AV's hum faded off as Alek felt himself drawn out of it and taken over the commons. Standing at the far end, he turned back toward the stage, in the near distance. The narrative voice called his attention to a middle-aged man in a straw hat and a younger woman, whose dark auburn hair was held back by a turquoise head band. "Directly in front of you are two journalists

Inauguration

who covered this event for the City Herald of New York," he heard the voice say.

After a pause, Marek Rankl's voice took over and greeted his audience. Over the next several minutes, Alek listened to the inaugural address for the first island nation of the Prometheus Frontier, Arête: that this was a unique moment in human history; that, historically, the well-known superpower far to the north had shown the way, as the first nation in history to enshrine reason, individual rights, and freedom—the keys to its unparalleled flourishing; that the founders of the Prometheus Frontier have learned from that history and have ensured that the Frontier's founding documents do not repeat its flaws or omissions; that the men and women on stage are the founding members of the Paine Society, chartered ten years ago *to begin the world over again*—a vision shared by all Arêteans here today; that the flame in the flag above is Arête's flame of reason and freedom, burning in the soul of every Arêtean; that this flame is now going to be brought into concrete existence—an actual, *physical* flame; that through all future generations, eras, and époques, it will be visible in the offshore waters of Arête City; that neither force of nature nor of man will ever extinguish it; that this flame will be as invincible as the heroic human spirit it symbolizes; that it will be the Prometheus Frontier's perpetual flame of reason and freedom.

Alek felt the breeze quicken as a sweeping applause began and spread across the commons. Everyone was now standing. He saw children jumping in place, unable to contain their energy.

Silence returned, however, as the stage emptied, and Alek saw the airspace above it take on a subtle shimmering effect. He knew that the audience, with no special equipment, was about to experience an ultra-immersion augmentation, and he also knew that he would be a part of it. They would all be consumed by the next portion of the program without moving from where they stood.

Inauguration

It commenced with the low rumble of powerful engines from somewhere under the stage. As the engines slowly ramped up, Alek felt his body being transported by an open craft on the Caribbean Sea. Salt spray filled his nostrils and found its way to his tongue as his eyes told him that, again, he was making for Arête City, small on the horizon. While he looked, he felt the vibrating craft through the soles of his feet, as its engines closed the distance.

A mile from the island, Alek saw the dark rock structure take shape. Near it, buoys signaled the presence of dangerous reefs. As the vessel slowed and drew closer again, he saw that the structure rose seventy-five feet out of the water. From its top a great flaring funnel, carved from black granite, reached for the sky. It was a modern-day fennel stalk—that makeshift torch in the ancient myth, fashioned by Prometheus to steal the divine fire—the fire that he would then bring to mankind.

As the craft slowed still further, its engines gave way to the roar of crashing waves and the shrieking of gulls. Alek, fully immersed in the drama, as he knew the entire audience was, experienced the sensation of wet skin; his hands went to his ears to quell the raucous cries of the birds. The roar of the waves intensified and then intensified further as it blended with the visual images—the rock structure, the water exploding against it, the wind-ripped sprays of salt.

Now the vessel was crawling as it drew ever closer to the rock structure—and then closer still. Alek, by force of will, broke the spell he was under, in order to observe the audience in front of him. All motion in the commons had come to a halt. It was as if everyone, their eyes on the approaching rock structure, had stopped breathing. Even the children were riveted in place, as their ears filled with the sound of thundering waves and shrieking gulls.

Inauguration

Finally, it happened. There was the superheated exhalation of a muted whoosh of blue flame bursting out of the funnel and into the sky. Alek caught the sweet scent of ignition, accompanied by a faint burning sensation in his nostrils; he could not help imagining that a giant hand had brought flint down against the torch's granite, to bring its flame to life.

He could not tell how long it took, but over the next several minutes, the great flame's color gradually warmed. At the same time, its initial height diminished and widened into large tongues of golden flame filling the granite funnel. Even in the morning's radiant sunlight, the flame was visible for miles around, waving in the wind and reaching fifty feet into the sky.

Finally, Alek realized that the stage had gone silent. But a large golden afterimage remained for long moments above it. Then gradually, it disappeared as well. He saw that the stage was empty, and he felt a warm soothing breeze caress his body. Another stage had been set—and lit.

But he saw one final image as the portal took him out of the commons and across the esplanade to the seawall. Spectators had already gathered there, looking at the perpetual flame. As he passed over them, a young woman with deep bronze hair and turquoise headband turned a radiant face up to him, as if she knew he was there.

Alek found himself back on Oribel, standing in front of the portal plate. Standing next to him, almost touching, he felt a presence—*Liang*.

"I didn't know you were with me," he said, looking into her eyes.

Inauguration

"All the way," she replied. A ray of sunlight found its way through the tropical foliage to her face—a face as radiant as it had been on the afternoon they met, five days ago.

The moment was a logical culmination and a new beginning. It was the culmination of a relationship which started that afternoon five days ago; it was the beginning of the rest of their life together. Hand in hand, saying nothing, they followed the nearby sound of waves heaving against the island's low cliffs. White longtails circled overhead. Alek and Liang entered the meadow where Armando Rojas's sculpture stood and walked to the nude bodies of Marek Rankl and Lenore Pellon. Never did those bodies look so alive.

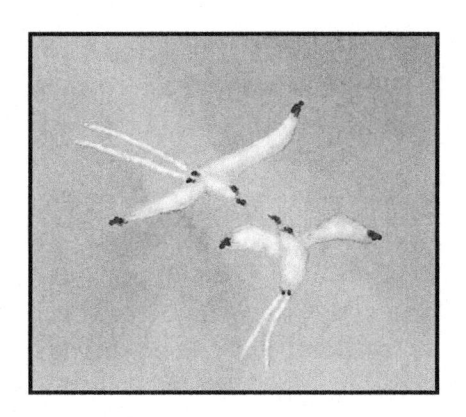

Between a black granite bench and the sculpture, thick moss covered the ground. They went to it and faced each other, still saying nothing, but their mouths had found each other now, as they knelt on the soft green bed, each of them reaching for the other's clothing but only to the extent necessary to bare what desperately needed to be bared, then she slowly rolling backward, her palms on each side of his face, gently, insistently, pulling him with her, her lips pulling his lips, and with her hands now guiding his hips and with their eyes locked, he slowly entered her body, the intensity and the intimacy of that action acutely sharpened by the fact that they were fully clothed; he said, Don't move, but she said, My body *has* to move, then he saw her lips part again and her eyes and mouth widen further, still looking into his eyes looking into hers, as their bodies shook in excruciating agony, her body continuing to spasm for long minutes after his, she with her hands still on his hips holding him captive within her, all the while looking into his eyes, and then his body responding again, pulsing in her body, to her *spirit*—and to *pleasure* which, like a life, is a reason unto itself.

EUDAIMONIA

Slowly the air vehicle lifted upward from the landing pad on Oribel. Liang was at the controls and Alek was beside her. It was the first day of his tour of Arête.

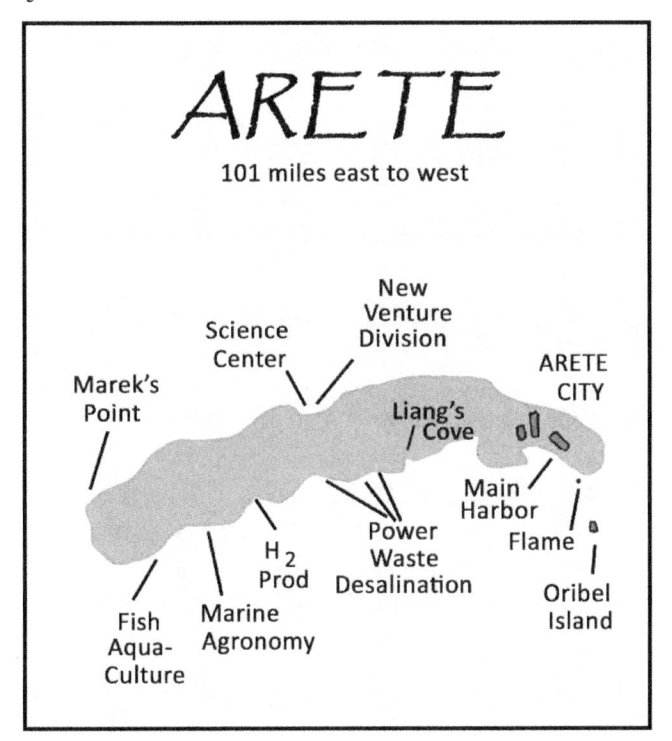

ARETE

101 miles east to west

- Marek's Point
- Science Center
- New Venture Division
- Liang's Cove
- ARETE CITY
- Main Harbor
- H_2 Prod
- Power Waste Desalination
- Flame
- Fish Aqua-Culture
- Marine Agronomy
- Oribel Island

He looked at her in the pilot's seat, her full attention on the controls. Sunglasses were perched on the top of her head, ready for use once they escaped the mountain's shadow. She brought the AV up to the level of the long room and waved its wings at

Eric and Rhee, still at the breakfast table. Then she banked and slowly headed for Arête.

She saw Alek looking at her and smiled. There was an ease to everything she did, made possible by a self-confidence that was second nature. Alek thought of what they had experienced in the sculpture garden yesterday and then a number of times during the night. Each time, her ultimate moments had become endless *minutes.* Those minutes, of which he had been so much a part, had enthralled him.

Now, as he watched her bring the vehicle to altitude and switch to auto-flight, he thought of Marek and Lenore, and how their lives had been extended. Had the secret of extending such ecstasy as Liang's also been discovered on Arête? He pointedly looked at her face. She turned to face him and, as if reading his mind, she smiled again, with an expression suggesting she knew what he had been thinking.

At breakfast, Eric had urged them to keep the pace relaxed during the tour. And Rhee, seeing their faces, could not resist adding that it should be a week punctuated by continued episodes of pure pleasure.

Eric had informed them that Marek and Lenore had made the entire island aware that Marek's great-grandson would be touring. They could expect invitations to lunches or dinners, and beach or yacht excursions. There would be simple end-of-day drinks and conversation. "You'll find that all island doors are open to you," Eric assured them.

During a leisurely flight to Arête, Liang told Alek that she had a loose itinerary in mind, one they could easily adjust in light of the unexpected. Today they would start with an aerial circumnavigation of Arête.

Eudaimonia

The perpetual flame came into view, with Arête one mile beyond. Liang dropped altitude and they paused a short distance from the flame. Even in full daylight, their faces reflected its moving tongues of flame. Alek thought of yesterday's portal and the augmented virtual reenactment of the flame's ignition seventy-five years ago. It was unchanged from that time, for it was designed *never* to change. He wondered what engineering feat made that possible but had no doubt that all contingencies had been anticipated.

They continued on at the same altitude and started to close the distance to the capital city. Weekend water activity dominated the blue green expanse below. Crafts of all shapes, sizes, and speeds were visible, with vivid colors sharing the water with more sedate pastels and whites.

Young bodies propelled themselves, upright, on battery powered surf boards. Others were prone on body boards, powered in the same way. Older bodies enjoyed enclosed pods favoring more modest speeds, with sudden, occasional bursts of high speed. There were many variations of traditional jet skiing, as well as water skiing behind speeding power boats. Yachts of various sizes were visible, as well as excursion boats.

In the air above, Alek saw large air taxis which Liang informed him would be heading to various parts of Arête, whether beaches, restaurants, or nature reserves. She told him that Arête had the largest bird sanctuary in the Caribbean, with exotic migratory species frequenting it from all parts of the globe. This was another of her passions, she told him.

As they drew nearer to the city, she aimed for the Arêtean flag, above the acoustic shell. But, before reaching it, she gently banked to port, to start a clockwise circuit of the island. She knew that the inauguration in yesterday's portal had already given him a close-up experience of the stage and commons.

Eudaimonia

Alek saw the seawall below. Multiple fishing lines glistened in the sun, and a man with a long rod was showing his young daughter how to surf-cast. On the esplanade there was a mix of roller boarders, cyclists, and motorized vehicles. The walkways edging each side of the wide avenue had a steady stream of foot traffic, the inner one more leisurely because of the many shops and galleries.

Liang brought them closer. He saw a number of old-fashioned bookstore-coffee shops and recalled that Arête was known throughout the world for resurrecting an ancient craft. It had established itself as the home for lavishly illustrated print books, of adult as well as children's literature.

Liang took them higher and then hovered. On the other side of the city, across the commons, Alek saw numerous high rises, intermingled with lower structures that Liang told him were largely administration and government buildings.

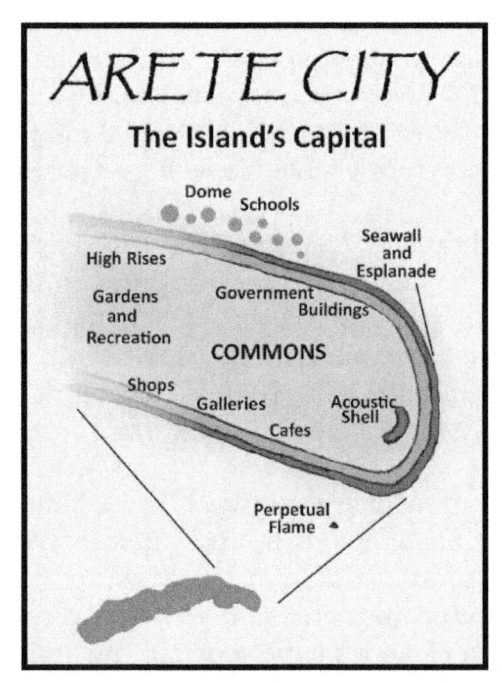

ARETE CITY
The Island's Capital

- Dome
- Schools
- Seawall and Esplanade
- High Rises
- Gardens and Recreation
- Government Buildings
- COMMONS
- Shops
- Galleries
- Cafes
- Acoustic Shell
- Perpetual Flame

Eudaimonia

Then as the AV slowly continued on, he occasionally glimpsed large geodesic globes behind the buildings. They were numerous.

When he asked about them, Liang increased altitude again, and he could see that they were actually floating islands a short distance off shore, behind the buildings. "Those globes are Arête's famous *Dome Schools*," she informed him.

She lowered altitude and again hovered. Alek noticed hilly paths, meandering flower gardens, and fishponds west of the commons. He saw a winding slide, similar to those in old water parks, running parallel to one of the paths and following its curves. Suddenly, he saw an older couple swooping down and then up to curve out of sight before plunging down again. Later, he remembered the sight of their outstretched hands reaching for the sky before they dropped from view. The image stuck in his mind, having captured the spirit of play so evident that morning. Then the AV again continued west, along the coast.

Liang's home was tucked into a small cove on the southern coast and up a hill on the forest's edge. The cove was ten miles west of Arête's main harbor. On the flat roof of her home, a landing pad connected to an AV hangar cut into the hill. Below, a deck, facing east, ran the full length of the living room and bedroom. She and Alek were enjoying breakfast on the deck. The night was a memory of the pleasure they had given each other, as were all the nights since their first one together on Oribel.

The tour, which was to last one week, had actually become two. They had spent time at each of RME's enterprises. The Marine Agronomy and Fish Aquaculture Divisions were on the southern coast, while the New Venture Division was on the northern.

Eudaimonia

In addition, the southern coast was the location for four large manufacturing operations, each an essential part of the island's infrastructure. The first of them was Arête's hydrogen production plant. This facility was one of the world's largest and most efficient producers of biohydrogen.

The hydrogen plant met all the island's energy needs. These included air vehicles, homes, and businesses, as well as the other three essential plants, for electric power, desalination, and waste management. These operations were centrally located on the island. Desalination was required even though Arête was water rich, with many rivers and aquifers. A steady supply of pure drinking water, not subject to the vagaries of climate, was an essential resource.

Alek was struck by the interconnectedness of everything that happened on the island. And he noted the key role of hydrogen as a biofuel whose sole byproduct was water. During the week, scientists he met stressed that everything RME achieved reflected its dependence on the utterly ubiquitous world of microbial life and the application of DNA supercomputing to it.

When Alek and Liang had visited *Marek's Point*, on the westernmost tip of Arête, this was brought home again. Microbiology was still Marek's first love, and he was now able to concentrate on it almost exclusively. On the lower level of his home, the door to his lab had a gold plaque reading *Methuselah*, the name associated with longevity. Inside, the lab's expansive windows looked out to where Earth's microbial life had originated billions of years before--the ocean.

Alek was especially intrigued by Marek's scientific breakthroughs in two areas. Yes, he assured Alek, through microbiology, it is possible to extend life and reverse aging. And yes again, it is possible to expand what he called *pillow pleasure*. He said the last with a smile as he looked at Lenore.

Eudaimonia

Life extension, he explained to Alek, involved exploring the intersection of two areas of research and building on and expanding what scientists had long known about those areas. The first area was human cell lines found to be immortal, meaning they do not age, but can proliferate indefinitely.

The other area was microbial. Science had gradually come to the realization that microbes are immortal in basically the same way. And this suggests, astoundingly, that the preponderance of life on Earth is immortal. Scientists estimate that the mass of microbes living beneath Earth's surface is more than twenty billion tons of carbon, a sum nearly four hundred times greater than the carbon mass of all humans.

Marek's innovations exhibited that for which he had become renowned throughout his life: gigantic inductive integrations, based upon ever increasing bodies of observed fact and scientific discovery.

At breakfast the next morning, they discussed the challenges Marek, and his team of scientists were facing. "But if I live long enough," he assured Alek, "we should at least be able to show the way beyond the new limits we have currently reached."

Hotels, private homes, and multi-dwelling buildings predominated on the north coast of Arête, along with many beaches—famous for their sand and surfing. The beaches were also ingress points to Arête's rainforests, with their trails, nature reserves, and occasional private homes.

Liang took Alek to her bird sanctuary, and other nature reserves as well. Throughout their tour of the island, Alek was struck by the attentive stewardship of the island's ecology. This was true of populated areas, as well as beaches and rainforests.

Eudaimonia

There was a reverence for nature and human-nonhuman interaction; it clearly pervaded the island.

"What makes that possible?" Alek asked.

"Simply paying attention," she replied. "And we are continually learning from Arête's many naturalists."

Midway on Arête's north coast, Rankl Marine Enterprises had located its New Venture Division. It comprised a spacious research center, science park, and museum. A large bay, occupying five miles of coastline, indented the island at that point. As with the other RME operations, a small city had grown up for homes, as well as medical, educational, and other professional services. This one was Ventura City. The two on the southern coast were Pisces and Agronom and, together, the three small cities were commonly referred to as the *Three Siblings*.

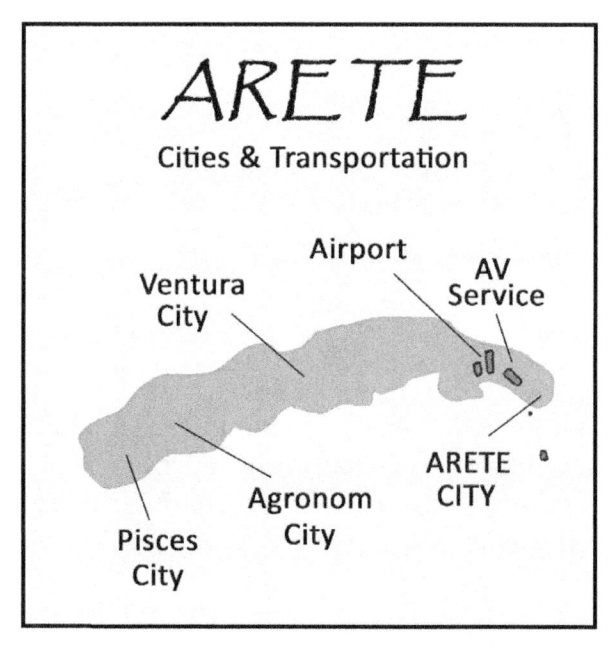

ARETE
Cities & Transportation

- Ventura City
- Airport
- AV Service
- Pisces City
- Agronom City
- ARETE CITY

East of Ventura, Liang continued along the northern coast toward Arête City, the capital. Approaching its outskirts,

Eudaimonia

however, they detoured to the south, over the forest. Arête's main harbor was on the southern coast, and Liang explained she wanted to approach it from the north.

A number of important features of the island were more readily visible from that direction.

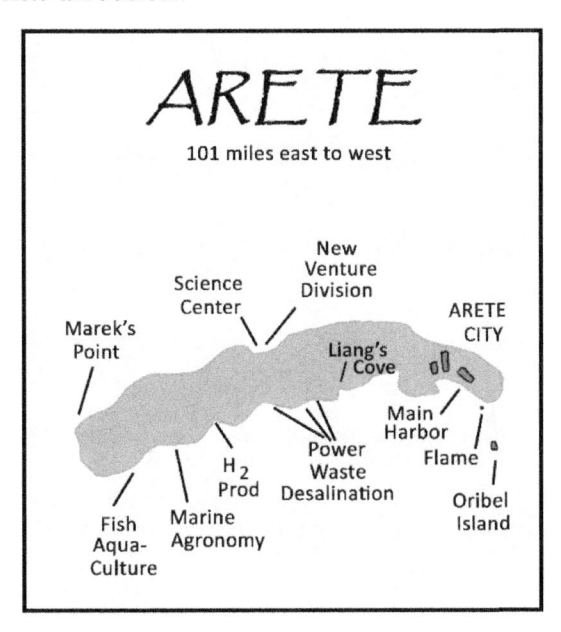

ARETE
101 miles east to west

- Marek's Point
- Science Center
- New Venture Division
- Liang's Cove
- ARETE CITY
- Main Harbor
- Flame
- Power Waste Desalination
- H_2 Prod
- Oribel Island
- Fish Aqua-Culture
- Marine Agronomy

Alek saw Arête's Airport, into which he had flown almost three weeks ago. South of that, the main harbor was visible with its many piers, cranes, and containers of all colors, waiting for their next destination. On the easternmost edge of the harbor, Liang pointed out a large facility which serviced all the island's many air vehicles. It was also the main hydrogen refueling point and home base for the many AV rental services. Other vehicles and machinery were serviced there as well, but, for transportation on Arête, the quiet, economical, and ubiquitous air vehicle, with its small, hydrogen powered engines, was the most popular.

From here, Liang headed back to the northern coast and continued following it into the capital city. She informed Alek that retired educators from many countries made their homes in the high rises, many of them enjoying second careers in the dome schools.

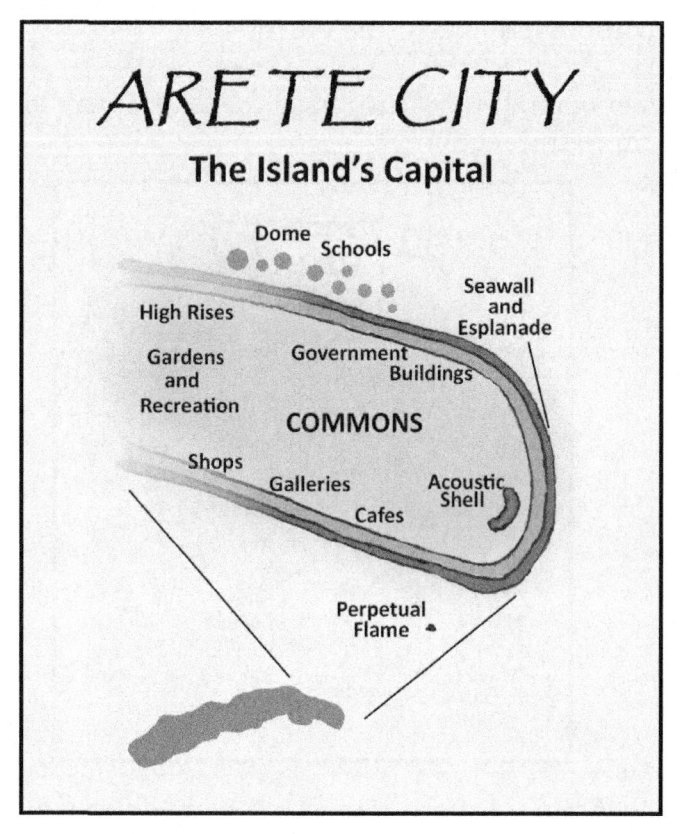

ARETE CITY
The Island's Capital

- Dome Schools
- High Rises
- Seawall and Esplanade
- Gardens and Recreation
- Government Buildings
- COMMONS
- Shops
- Galleries
- Cafes
- Acoustic Shell
- Perpetual Flame

Further into Arête City, they visited various government buildings dealing with legislation, courts, and police. One building especially interested Alek. This was the Foundation building. He knew from the ninth portal that two chief roles of the Foundation were adjudication of constitutional issues and management of the Frontier's defenses.

The Foundation also coordinated much of what happened in the government from an administrative standpoint. But with the complete separation of government and private sector, all business activity throughout the Frontier, without exception, was in private hands. "Attempts to give government even a simple coordinating role in the economy—this idea occasionally rears its head—are especially shunned," Liang explained to Alek.

"A slippery slope area," he said.

"Sure is."

Alek's tour was complete. Sitting at breakfast on Liang's deck, he reached for the binoculars on the table. He first looked east to Arête and then trained them on the perpetual flame in Arête's harbor. Nine miles south of the flame, he could see the island of Oribel.

Then he put the glasses down and looked at Liang. "You know I can't imagine life without you," he said.

"I know, my love. Nor can I without you."

They stood at the deck railing then, leaning against one another. Each felt the heat of the other's existence. Alek Rankl looked again to the torch, this time with his naked eyes, and realized it was the source of the heat they felt. Her world was his world now—indeed it was *their* world. He knew, with utter certainty, that she felt the same way.

Each of them was looking to the flame. They felt themselves bonded by its heat, its light, but more than anything, by what it represented.

Suddenly, Alek felt a change in Liang's body. She lunged for the binoculars and trained them on the flame. Even without the binoculars, he could see that the flame had changed. It had increased in height, and its color was a continuous pulsing red. "What is it?" he demanded.

"What you see is the code for the worst type of attack," Liang responded, her voice filled with alarm. "At the rate of the pulse, it means the worst type of category four attack—a *bio* attack. We've been hit."

CRISIS

The air vehicle lifts off from Liang's rooftop landing pad and banks toward Arête City. Their destination is the Foundation building, which also houses the Frontier's Defense Department. The Emergency War Council is about to convene.

An Island News feed comes on the AV's sound system. "This is Emma Lane reporting from the capital city's hospital with the latest on the category four bio emergency. Given the grotesque severity of what we are seeing, the island must assume the worst-case scenario—that we are the victim of a bio weapon attack. As we speak, Arête's Emergency War Council is convening. Please stay tuned for the Island News team's round-the-clock emergency coverage."

An incoming call replaces Emma's voice. It is Marek. "Liang, Alek," he orders, "get over to the City Hospital. Emma Lane is expecting you. She has been gathering facts already, and no journalist is better at it than she is."

When they arrive at the hospital, Alek is amazed that she looks no older than she did in the recent portal presentation he went through of Arête's inauguration, even though that inauguration was seventy-five years ago. "What you are about to see is a scene you'll never forget," she warns them. "So be prepared. I myself have never witnessed such horror. Historically, hemorrhagic fever has a 50% kill rate. For this one, it's 90%. Death is unimaginably horrible—all internal and external body orifices bleed out. There is little that can be done, it all happens so quickly."

Crisis

The corridor is filled with gurneys holding the victims, whose bodies are swathed in white sheets, most blood-soaked. Many have already died. Liang sees a young girl on a gurney, alone. She seems familiar, and Liang is horrified when she hears barely audible words coming from the child's blood encrusted lips. The young child recognizes Liang and reaches for her, softly pleading "Ling Ling, Ling Ling."

Emma lunges at Liang and pulls her back, warning, "Far too contagious. Not even the poor thing's parents are allowed near her."

Liang turns away, shocked.

Emma, Liang, and Alek find an empty cafeteria table and sit. Emma tells them, "I interviewed a number of bereaved families last night and this morning. When I asked them about their recent movements, a clear pattern emerged. For a number of families, their movements included a visit to Arête's bird sanctuary in the rainforest not far from the capital city. I think this is something for Arête's Infectious Disease Command."

Marek Rankl and Dr Allan Oh are at the bird sanctuary's Koi pond. They had received Emma's report with great interest, and this interest increases immediately upon arrival at the bird sanctuary. They see an employee flinging fistfuls of pellet food into the Koi pond and the water churning with feeding fish. Each man knows that most infectious disease in the tropics is water borne, and they go directly to the worker feeding the fish. Oh says, "Excuse me, I'm from Infectious Disease and I need a handful of that food." The young man looks quizzically at him, and Marek says, "It is okay, son, he is with me." He looks at Marek and says, "Hello, Mr Rankl, of course." Oh grabs a handful of pellets and inspects them with his eye loupe. "I don't see anything suspicious," he says, "but I want a lab analysis."

Crisis

Emma Lane and Dr Allan Oh are in conversation at the Island News Team emergency desk. Emma turns to the camera and addresses her audience.

"This is Emma Lane with the latest on the category four bio emergency. All Arête hospitals are overwhelmed. But a major breakthrough was made today. We now know what we will be dealing with in the weeks ahead. With me is Dr Allan Oh, the head of Arête's Infectious Disease Command. Dr Oh, would you please summarize for us."

"Yes, certainly. We now know beyond any doubt that this calamity is not an accidental event. Rather we know that we have been attacked by the deadliest type of weapon—a bio weapon. A bio weapon is unmatched in its evil and in its ability to destroy human life. We have established that we are dealing with a large mosquito from Southeast Asia which has been weaponized by infecting it with a hemorrhagic fever virus and then releasing it in great numbers over Arêtean air space. This mosquito is physically distinctive by bright red bands encircling its legs.

"The virus is the deadliest hemorrhagic fever virus I have ever encountered, now airborne over Arête and threatening her very existence. Each female mosquito—only the female bites us—has become a weapon, ready to inject a deadly disease into whomever she bites, with a nearly one hundred percent success rate. Thousands of such weapons have been unleashed over Arête—each an agent of death—a *ghastly* death.

"Dr Oh, please explain how this was pulled off," Emma Lane interjects. "This is such a powerful and deadly weapon in a relatively tiny carrier, a mosquito."

"The design, though diabolical, is ingenious," Oh replies, "with three components." Then for the next five minutes, with

Crisis

the aid of visuals depicting the biology of the weapon, Dr Oh describes its components.

"First is for scientists to produce blood infected with a deadly virus. This is the easy part, by contrast to the problem of weaponizing a mosquito with that virus. Second is the existence of fish food in the form of dry pellets. This is another easy part. Fish food has long been common in pellet form. Third, mosquito egg pellets with hard protective shells, like fish food pellets. Now this is the hard part. Mosquitoes with pellet shaped, rigid eggs are not common," Oh points out. "But the Red-Banded Mosquito of Southeast Asia is a species which does. *This* is the key component of the bio weapon."

"And that's where the Bird Sanctuary outside of Arête City comes in?" Emma Lane asks.

"Yes. Fish food pellets used at the sanctuary's Koi pond were found to be comingled with Red-Banded Mosquito egg pellets. Now here's the key: The Red-Banded Mosquito egg pellets had been carefully collected in the wild and taken to a bio weapon facility where they were injected with blood containing the deadly virus. When these pellets are later flung into water, such as the Koi Pond of Arête's bird sanctuary, many voraciously hungry larvae, upon hatching, find a delectable blood meal ready for them.

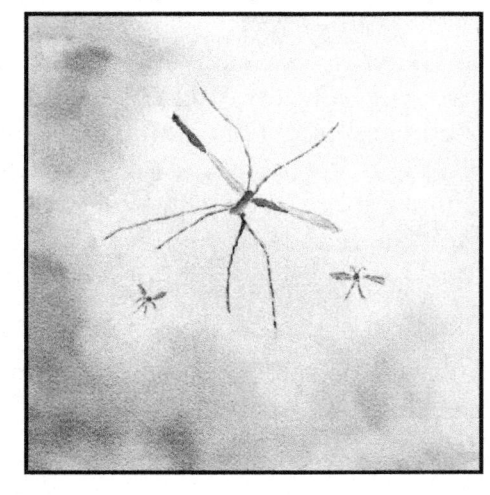

"Now think of it. This blood meal is contaminated with the deadly virus, and after being consumed by the mosquito larvae, that virus continues to an inactive pupae stage and from there into adult mosquitoes. And what you see next," Oh concludes, "is thousands of adult female mosquitoes—only the females bite us—launched over the population of Arête. A deadly bio weapon is now airborne."

"A ghastly nightmare scenario," Emma says.

"Yes, it is," Oh agrees, "**but vitally imp**ortant, are two things for our listeners to realize. First, we now know *what* we are dealing with. Without that we could not even get started defending ourselves.

Second, we know that it is caused by humans, and when we identify them—which we will—we will be able to put a stop to their evil—for good.

"In the meantime," Emma asks, "what immediate actions can Arêteans take to protect themselves?"

"Two things. First: Spray your body liberally with the insect spray. It has been made available in large quantities throughout the island. Second: Keep your insect swatters, of whatever type, at the ready. Arm each family member with them. You need to do both. Neither is sufficient by itself. Throughout the island, we are making spray and swatters available in large quantities. Think of the spray as your body armor and the swatter as your sword."

"In other words, it's hand to hand combat," Emma interjects.

"Yes, at the ground level, that's exactly what it is," Oh agrees.

"Dr Allan Oh, thank you."

"You are most welcome."

The Emergency War Council is convened in Arête City's Foundation building. The war room is basically round and approximately thirty feet in diameter. Its continuous wall is an off-white color.

Marek Rankl sits at the head of a rectangular table. The other eight council members sit at the table's two longer sides. Arête's flag stands behind Marek and off to one side, near the wall.

Alek and Liang are next to each other, and Liang whispers to him, "By constitution, Marek heads the War Council, as senior member of the Foundation."

"Ladies and gentlemen, let us begin," Marek says. "I want to commence with points of order. This war council consists of four voting members: Dray Blackwood, overall director of frontier defense, Davesh Navendra, cyber defense, Lenore Pellon, intellectual defense, and me. In addition, there are five non-voting members, randomly selected from Arête's general population. We have a lot to get done today. Time is of the utmost importance. Arête's very survival is at stake."

It is a quiet residential street but for emergency sirens in the near distance. One siren intensifies as a large helicopter appears, and lands near the front door of a home.

The pilot, in protective gear, dashes for the house. A grim-faced man stands in the doorway, his young son wrapped around his leg, wailing. His wailing increases as the pilot and the man load a body bag, containing the boy's mother, into the helicopter.

Other sirens in the distance fluctuate in intensity until, finally, quiet returns.

Crisis

A fumigation helicopter approaches a pond. The pilot, wearing a protective mask, hovers above the water. He glances at his control panel and checks the wind before dropping to eight feet above the water.

Immediately he proceeds to spray. A white billowing cloud trails under the helicopter. Then he does the foliage around the pond, changing altitude multiple times as he circles it, to ensure coverage.

Over another residential area, an emergency helicopter is blaring out a warning. "Do not ... repeat ... do *not* ... touch your infected family members. They are victims of a deadly bleeding disease. You must keep them isolated until an emergency vehicle arrives to either deliver a body bag or take them to hospital. Victims dead or alive are highly contagious. You yourself will surely become another victim if you so much as touch any body fluid."

Other emergency helicopters are making the same announcement in the distance.

In a remote rainforest area, heavy earth-moving equipment is excavating a large pit for an open-air crematorium, in an area where all trees and brush have been removed. Construction workers, a man and a woman, each wearing a hard hat, are on the side, observing. "Terrible the loss of life we are seeing," he says to her. "Yes," she replies. "This is the safest way to dispose of the diseased remains of the victims. There are so many already and so many more expected."

It is evening, and an exhausted Emma Lane, dark circles under her eyes, is at the Island News Team emergency desk. A cacophony of sounds, subdued, but very much present, fills the studio's ambient air: a drumbeat of war, earth-moving equipment, emergency helicopter sirens and their megaphones.

Crisis

But her eyes are on her audience. "Day Two of the bio attack on our island is coming to a close," she begins. "The entire island is mobilized, but at times, the odds against us seem insurmountable. The totally unexpected nature of the bio attack seems to have gotten the jump on us.

"But we can take heart in the fact that the path out of this nightmare is defined and engages each and every one of us. The intense action required of us is what will enable us to maintain our sanity now that our paradise has become such a hell. There is no such thing as hopelessness on our island. Not now. Not ever. This is the message of the man who is going to address us now, Marek Rankl."

Marek replaces Emma on screen and wastes no time. He too shows signs of exhaustion, but those signs are secondary to the calm sense of command he exudes, as he begins speaking.

"Thank you, Emma. My dear fellow Arêteans, our island nation is undergoing the greatest challenge since its founding seventy-five years ago. Our very survival is at stake, but *we will survive.*

"You have seen the Infectious Disease Command's containment plan—Incineration, Fumigation, Isolation. But to fully defeat this bio weapon—a deadly weaponized mosquito—it is necessary—indeed it is unavoidable—that each Arêtean enters the field of battle: man, woman, boy, girl. Each of us must be ready to do physical hand to hand combat, so to speak, or be involved in supporting those who do."

It is early morning of day four. The Emergency War Council is convened in the Foundation building's War Room. Various video loops stream onto the twelve segments of the War Room's continuous wall. Each panel is six feet wide and presents a different portion of the besieged Arête: the containment measures, the helicopters, the fire pits, the wailing bystanders—all to the whining drone of mosquitoes and the drumbeat of war. The cacophony of sound is subdued, however, as Marek starts speaking.

"We are now in day four of the crisis," he begins. "On the island, the concentration is on measures taken to minimize the loss of life. These are the containment activities streaming to the display panels all around us. But now we are going to dim the lights and actually enter the field of battle, to directly experience this unspeakable atrocity."

The lights go out and different video loops come onto the room's continuous wall panels. In the dim room, they come into sharp relief. The nine War Council members, wearing virtual headsets, find themselves in the thick of battle. They are surrounded by it and aware of nothing else. The sounds of the battlefield have intensified: the whine of mosquitoes, the sound of swatters, adult voices of encouragement and voices of warning.

There is the heart-stopping cry of a ten-year-old boy who is bitten, despite his body spray, "Dad. I've been bit!," followed by his mother's shrieking, "Noooooooooo!" Underlying it all is the haunting drumbeat of war, intensifying as the battle sounds intensify.

The war room is a world where chaos and insanity would seem to rule.

But the thick of the battle reaches a peak, and its sounds reach a crescendo—then both taper off. Island medical personnel in Cat 4 protective gear secure the dead in body bags and load them into large helicopters, for transport to cremation sites. The large fire pits, taped off, are continually blazing.

There is a fire pit with family members watching, many of them elderly, their faces aglow from the flames, wailing as they gaze from the outside perimeter. There is another site at which

Crisis

family members, many with children, stand vigil in complete silence.

Three fast video clips of a special force operation are also looping. In the first clip, a lithe, powerful figure, in scuba gear, comes up behind an enemy diver under water, slashes through his oxygen tube and then through his throat.

In another, a figure in black is patrolling the rainforest outside the RME science center. This figure hurls a four-pointed Japanese shuriken deep into an attacker's right eye socket.

In the last clip, a smaller figure, with a wide black headband, is grabbed from behind but instantly twists free and delivers an elbow strike that crushes the attacker's windpipe.

A final clip reveals these defenders. Armando, Liang, and Alek are squatting in a huddle, their heads almost touching, Armando still in underwater gear, Liang wearing a wide black headband.

Finally, the War Room's lights are back on, and everyone simply sits in place, unable to move or speak or even to weep—too *drained*.

Reese Ransome, deep blue eyes moist, is the first to speak. "If I live to a thousand, I don't think I could ever forget this."

"Nor do I," Emma Lane concurs. "And I will surely spend the rest of my days making sure that the world never forgets it either. But tell me, someone, what is that special op sequence all about?"

"We have Alek to thank for that," Marek replied. "Once he saw that we were developing a generic vaccine to ensure our survival, he asked whether Helix had been programmed to detect asymmetric attacks on our virology center.

"Davesh and his team wrote a special program for Helix to probe for suspicious activity in the waters surrounding Arête

Crisis

Island. They then tweaked that program to focus deeply on the north shore waters of Arête, in the vicinity of Ventura City. He found that such an attack was actually already in progress. If it succeeded in taking out our science center, it could clinch the end of the Prometheus Frontier.

"And finally, with another thank you to Helix, we have conclusive evidence of who orchestrated the current crisis. It will surprise no one in this room that Pangaia is the perpetrator. The evidence is incontestable. With that evidence, we know what actions we need to take in order to ensure this atrocity never recurs.

"Careful deliberation, however, must take place first. We must act fast, but the voting members must be unanimous on each action and, with Reese Ransome coordinating, any concern of non-voting members must be considered as well."

It is late afternoon on day five of the crisis. Reese Ransome and the eight other council members file into the War Room and take their seats.

"The long break," she begins, was for our five non-voting members to have one last opportunity to weigh in on the decisions we had come to today. These are the decisions regarding what actions the Frontier needs to take against Pangaia. As the lead of the non-voting members, I can report to the war council that we have no concerns."

"Thank you," Marek says. "From this point, we proceed as follows. There are three actions. First Action: Completely and immediately shut down Pangaia and render Pangaia Island totally nonfunctional. Second: Demand reparation. Finally: Address the global uproar that is sure to result."

Crisis

It is five minutes before midnight, and most buildings on Pangaia Island are dimly lit for the usual staff of nighttime employees. Also subdued at this hour is New York's skyline, in the near distance.

Pangaia's night security officer is sitting on a lawn chair outside his office, taking it all in. Suddenly, an emergency message flashes, with shrill beeps, from the computer in the office. He rushes in and sees Marek Rankl about to talk.

"This emergency message," Rankl starts, "is for Pangaia General Secretary, Galea Magre, and for Pangaia Island Security. Pangaia Island in New York harbor goes dark in five minutes time. All power will be gone. All backup generators will be dead.

"Pangaia headquarters in New York harbor will be no more. At midnight, all its buildings, electronic infrastructure, servers, wireless networks, data repositories, communication equipment will shut down and be rendered permanently unusable.

"Complete evacuation of nighttime employees will start immediately and must finish by 2:00 AM. To expedite evacuation, the battery-powered transportation pods will be left unscathed until 2:00 AM. Pathway lights will remain on until 2:00 AM as well.

"There will be no loss of life.

"But there will be complete and permanent destruction of Pangaia Island as the world knows it.

"There is nothing that will stop it or delay it. Pangaia's days in the western hemisphere are over."

Crisis

Galea Magre is in her living room, dressed for bed. She stands, riveted, in front of the large screen of her entertainment center. She is listening to the same address by Marek Rankl to which her security officer is listening. Marek Rankl is just finishing.

"Oh my god, oh my god, oh my god, Marek Rankl," Magre exclaims, her voice choked.

On Pangaia Island, all the buildings have gone dark. The lights of the transportation pods and the lamps along the island walkways remain as the only sources of artificial light—for evacuation.

It is evening of the next day, and Emma Lane is broadcasting from the Island News Team emergency desk.

"Good evening, Arêteans. This is the fifth day of war and of our battle for survival in the face of a diabolical bio attack. The vaccine has been received by most Arêteans and is expected to be complete for all of Arête tomorrow.

"Last night, at midnight, the Prometheus Frontier took action against Pangaia, the orchestrator of this hideous attack. Through our unmatched cyber power, the Frontier has totally and permanently shut down Pangaia Island. The island was evacuated by 2:00 AM with no loss of life.

"Our evidence of Pangaia's culpability for the bio attack is incontestable and will be made known to the entire world. For now, I will simply report that the initial uproar against the Frontier for the shutdown of Pangaia Island is enormous."

"We go now to the War Room, from which Marek Rankl will address the world, live."

Crisis

Marek sits alone at the head of the table. He is dressed as he has been since the start of the crisis. His face is fatigued, almost haggard, his hair somewhat disheveled. But his head is high, and he projects an enormous inner calm.

"This is Marek Rankl addressing the world from the seat of Arête's government, housed in our capital city's Foundation building. The island nation of Arête has been under siege for the past five days. The immediate agent of death is a deadly mosquito that humans have weaponized to wreak havoc on Arête. Their intention: the complete annihilation of Arête's population.

"Rest assured, first of all, that this is not going to happen. We have already broken the back of this bio weapon and recovery is underway.

"Just as important, we now know, with absolute certainty, that Pangaia, Earth's one-world organization, is the orchestrator of this unspeakable atrocity. Consider its meaning. Pangaia has launched a monumental evil against the most peaceful and benevolent nation the world has ever seen.

"Rest assured that we will be making public the evidence of Pangaia's culpability for the entire world to see.

"At first it seemed that we were doomed, so sudden was the attack, so diabolical the design, so rapid its spread once launched. Images of the devastation have saturated all international news outlets.

"But Arête has survived, we will recover, and we will be stronger than ever.

"We invite liberty groups throughout the world to join us in our cause—the cause of reason and freedom. We invite them, we *welcome* them, to make our flag, emblazoned with the perpetual flame of reason and freedom, their own.

Crisis

"The bio attack on Arête makes it crystal clear, to the world's liberty lovers, the nature of our enemy and the depth of its evil."

The next day, Reese Ransome sits at her desk in Arête City's Foundation building, hands gently clasped in front of her. Arête's flag stands behind her desk and to the side. Her deep blue eyes look into the camera.

"Good Day. Yesterday evening, Marek Rankl, addressed the world regarding the shutdown of Pangaia's headquarters in New York harbor. Today, I, Reese Ransome, Legal Director of the Prometheus Frontier Foundation, do hereby levy the following two articles against Pangaia—one of reparation, one of punishment—for its unspeakably heinous bio attack on the Prometheus Frontier.

"Article One: As reparation, Pangaia will immediately cede ownership of New York harbor's Pangaia Island to the Prometheus Frontier.

"Article Two: As punishment, Pangaia, the world organization, whether it keeps that shameful name or not, is henceforth banished from ever again establishing headquarters in the western hemisphere.

"These articles are not open to negotiation. They are not open to discussion. The Prometheus Frontier will ever stand ready to enforce both articles."

UNLIMITED FUTURE

Emma Lane is broadcasting from the Island News Team emergency desk.

"Good afternoon Arêteans. We have now lived through ten days of Arête in crisis. I am happy to report that, although the memory of the bio attack will always be with us, a reminder that evil forces ever exist that would have us gone, this crisis is over. As Marek Rankl stated, with time, we will fully recover and do so with a renewed and greater strength. To augment this, the moral support of the Frontier's friends is ever a constant.

"The Frontier has always advanced the well-being of the nations with which it trades. It enriches the entire Caribbean region, and then the world at large, with its productive enterprises, global commerce, and employment opportunities. Its environmental recovery processes restore degraded lands, waters, and reefs. Its fish aquaculture processes offset the effects of overfishing and enable threatened species to flourish again in Earth's oceans. And its marine agronomy processes advance nutrition throughout the world, at the same time revolutionizing hydrogen production as the leading bio fuel driving Earth's engines—its sole byproduct: pure water.

"The Prometheus Frontier stands as a beacon to the world of what is possible when initiated physical coercion is constitutionally banished from all its affairs, both public and private.

"Unfortunately, many nations take the Frontier's phenomenal success as a reproach, and they would have us gone. This is

Unlimited Future

what drives Pangaia. Pangaia is infused with hatred of the good and hence of Arête whose very name means *excellence*. The bio attack on Arête made this reality crystal clear to the entire world.

"The world now sees Pangaia in its true colors. Vocal liberty groups throughout the world never miss an opportunity to speak for all the Arêtean men, women, and children who, because of Pangaia's monstrous attack, are never again to walk her sands or swim her waters.

"The worldwide furor against the Frontier's actions is reversed and is now a worldwide furor against Pangaia's evil. What is the result? Complete capitulation to the Frontier's demands. Pangaia officially cedes Pangaia Island to the Frontier. Pangaia officially acknowledges that it is henceforth banished from ever again establishing headquarters in the western hemisphere."

———

Marek Rankl, Lenore Pellon, Armando Rojas, Alek Rankl, and Joan Liang are on Liang's deck. Hors d'oeuvres, chilled glasses, and celebratory bottles of champagne are on the deck table.

The sun has just disappeared below the horizon and the western sky is a luminous gold. In the eastern sky, billowing cumulus clouds, by reflection, are alive with the same golden glow, beneath which, the perpetual flame is waving, itself ever golden, in the offshore waters of Arête City.

"This is my favorite color, the sky as it is now," Marek says, sweeping his hand across the sky, radiant gold in the East and West, with long feathery, golden wisps between.

Lenore looks at him and says, "Gold."

"Yes," he answers, "Gold."

Unlimited Future

"This is why your yacht, Oribel, has always been gold," Liang says.

"Yes," Marek responds. "But it is more than the radiant sky before us at this moment. The glory of the sky at this moment is short-lived."

"Fugitive," Armando adds.

"Yes, Old Friend, stunning skies are always fugitive. What I have in mind is *not* fugitive."

"You mean the perpetual flame," Alek says.

"Yes."

All on the deck are now gazing out to the golden flame in the near distance. They are stopped in time—each of them united in a great venture—a great venture known as The Prometheus Frontier. Finally its founder, Marek Rankl, speaks to the source—the source of that greatness.

"Yes," he declares, "I mean the gold which is the perpetual flame of reason and freedom. Never to be extinguished—always our beacon—and the world's—to an unlimited future."

THE END

EPILOGUE

As time unfolds, the million square miles of fair Caribbean Sea grows ever fairer, and in the process, continues to enrich the world at large.

Scientists are attracted to an environment where private capital and private initiative drive research—and not the government. Retirees are drawn to an educational system offering a dynamic interaction—that between their accumulated wisdom and the boundless curiosity of youthful minds.

Arête's new government has built a vital new principle into its constitution. This principle is The Primacy of the Declaration of Freedom. It resoundingly declares that all constitutional articles, clauses, and amendments, in perpetuity, must be fully subservient to and consistent with the original Declaration of Freedom.

Other Caribbean islands observe the Frontier and seek to emulate it. If they fully adopt and implement the Declaration, success is possible. Otherwise, it is not. The Paine Society, with its charter *To begin the world over again*, stands ever ready to guide and assist. Its charter is a perpetual one.

Lenore Pellon and Joan Liang coauthor the book, *Slippery Slope: a History*, to demonstrate that deviation from the Declaration of Freedom unavoidably leads to cronyism, dependence, and pressure group warfare. Their book is a timeless influence.

Epilogue

Arête's first party is the *Constitution Party*. But it was known from the start that another party would be needed. In the natural course of events, even with reason as the ultimate authority, there are honest disagreements about how best to govern. Such disagreements are compounded as the Frontier expands to other island nations. The Frontier eventually becomes a federation of islands, and a second party is born—the *Federation Party*.

The *Constitution Party* concentrates on the vision advanced by the Declaration of Freedom. The *Federation Party* concentrates on the complexities of governing to that vision as the Frontier expands to other islands and cultures.

For each party, fidelity to the Declaration of Freedom is sacrosanct. Each develops its own platform, with differences in emphasis. For any disagreement over the Declaration's basic philosophy, whether within a party or between parties, reason is ever the ultimate guide—and authority—to resolution.

Shortly after Pangaia's banishment, the NYC Police Department finds the bound and bloodless body of Galea Magre in her condominium. When Emma Lane accesses the crime scene report, it is clear to her what has happened. The dried remains of two large mosquitoes, with bright red bands encircling their spindly legs, had been found behind Magre's living room drapes. A quick Helix search confirmed what Emma already suspected. A vindictive Gina Pudaro had paid Magre a visit when it became evident that her old friend had exposed her to the authorities.

When Pangaia cedes ownership of its island to the Prometheus Frontier, the Frontier renames it *Prometheus Island*. All buildings are imploded, and the rubble removed. No longer is the island to have the shape of the ancient supercontinent after

Epilogue

which it had been named. It is re-sculpted back to its original form, that of New York's Governors Island.

The capstone project is the construction on the island of the *Prometheus Institute of Capitalism* which looks out upon the restored Statue of Liberty, a short distance away. Emma Lane scripts a docudrama of these events, a film which never fails to captivate visitors to Liberty Island's media center. It is titled *The Great Banishment*, after the event which had cleared the way.

Marek & Lenore leave legacies that immeasurably enrich the Prometheus Frontier. Each legacy is the product of a lifetime doing what they most love doing. For him it is research into the endlessly fascinating world of microbes. And for her it is the endlessly captivating world of philosophy.

Eric and Rhianna Rankl spend a great many years at Marek's Point where they happily immerse themselves in the Methuselah Project. Through Methuselah, many Frontier citizens enjoy extended lives and extended pillow pleasure. The Rankls establish that achieving success, in either realm, is equally a product of human volition as it is of following prescribed protocols.

Emma Lane, so taken by the flame ignited at Arête's inauguration, happily lives out her long, pleasured life doing intellectual battle for the Frontier. At the end, propped up in bed, she expresses a last wish. Her life partner, Reese Ransome, throws open the shutters wide and places a turquoise headband around her beloved's forehead. It contrasts with her still deep-bronze hair. Then hand in hand, their eyes take them over the offshore water of Arête City to the perpetual flame, waving in the tropical breeze. Emma thinks to herself what she has always thought during such moments, that the flame truly *is* a living

Epilogue

thing. Her headband matches the intermixed blues and greens of the infinitely beckoning Caribbean Sea, and Emma Lane's spirit becomes one with the flame.

Alek Rankl and Davesh Navendra enjoy a deep and productive friendship for many years. They learned from Pangaia's bio weapon attack. It had been a close brush with disaster. With that experience, they perfect Alek's algorithm for integrating surprise and deception into a defense system and then they integrate *that* integration with Helix, the foundation of the Frontier's hard defense. Lenore and Liang integrate it into the Frontier's intellectual defense system as well, to Alek's great pleasure.

Alek & Liang Rankl live longest of all. Their many offspring ensure the Rankl line in the Frontier through the millennia.

Armando Rojas is immortalized by the timeless artistic creations he leaves behind. These include the Frontier's unique martial arts program, the *Rojas System*.

The renown of the Prometheus Frontier leads many of the world's islands to join its federation of islands. On Earth's continents, metaphorical islands form as well. Regions and towns, or states and provinces seeking to live by the Frontier's Declaration of Freedom—its philosophy, its *spirit*—become virtual islands of freedom.

The Paine Society ever pursues the vision that, with enough of these virtual islands in place, conceivably even earth's advanced and largely coercive nations could "begin the world over again" and become part of the Prometheus Frontier.

Through the millennia, the wonders of science continue to enrich and expand human life. Science makes it possible to

Epilogue

replace all body parts, while consciousness and mind and their seemingly miraculous processes persistently remain the subject of research, ever beckoning to be further understood and elucidated.

The Prometheus Frontier flourishes year after year, century after century, millennium after millennium. It never wants for friends and allies.

On planet Earth, a perpetual flame continues to burn in the offshore waters of an enchanted Caribbean island. *Arête*. Ever does this flame stand for reason and freedom. And ever does it stand sentinel to the perpetual conflict of freedom versus coercion.

The Prometheus Frontier remains vigilant and ready. Never does it forget that, at any moment, rational beings have the power of volition—the power to choose *un*reason -- to choose *not* to think--but instead, initiate physical coercion to try to achieve their goals.

Epilogue

An ancient papyrus is preserved within a granite vault off the main lobby of Arête City's Foundation building. It forecasts the struggle leading to the Prometheus Frontier and the struggle that will ever continue between freedom and coercion. The papyrus is Aeschylus's lost drama, *Gaia's War*. A famous calligrapher excerpted its final words and burned them into the exterior granite of the vault.

> Prometheus perpetually battles Gaia and her forces of coercion. These are the forces seeking to subject rational beings and harness them into slavery.
>
> And Prometheus's reward for battling Gaia is great. He sees the future of a frontier that carries his name. And he sees it flourishing for all time in a most excellent place.
>
> The Prometheus Frontier

THE PROMETHEUS FRONTIER

About the Author

Kevin Osborne

Writer/artist Kevin Osborne lives in Farmington CT with his wife, Judith Stewart. www.PrometheusConnection.com spotlights his two Prometheus books. He is also the author and illustrator of *Mutekikon,* a 2010 fable, available on DVD. Trailer: www.mutekikon.com. Request DVD directly from the author. $5 with shipping. Payment not required in advance.

Contact Info: ko@mutekikon.com

About the Editor

Alex Bleier

Alex Bleier, editor of The Prometheus Connection and The Prometheus Frontier, works out of Colorado Springs in the beautiful Rocky Mountains. With degrees in Math, Philosophy, and Technical Communication, his extensive career in computer consulting has spanned the gamut from Fortune 500 companies to Silicon Valley startups. He currently concentrates on Internet systems development, search engine optimization, Internet marketing, eCommerce, and Amazon print-on-demand / Kindle book publishing.

Contact Info: alexbleiertech@gmail.com

THE PROMETHEUS FRONTIER

Acknowledgements

In the writing of this novel there were many influences, and upon reflection, I see that they fall into four categories: the editorial, the philosophic, the literary, and the inspirational.

The chief editorial force was Alex Bleier, who also edited my nonfiction prequel to this novel—*The Prometheus Connection*. What I said about Alex there applies to this book as well. Quite simply, *The Prometheus Frontier* would not be before your eyes now but for the steady illuminating force of Alex Bleier. Format and verbal flourishes in this book's Declaration of Freedom owe their existence to Thomas Jefferson's Declaration of Independence—my nods to a great achievement. Special mention goes out to Deb & Adam Mocciolo who touched every chapter with their careful readings, observations, questions, and suggestions—all invaluable. Finally, thanks go to Jon Hersey, managing editor of The Objective Standard who touched, for the better, early drafts of the prologue and the first three chapters.

As to philosophic influence, foremost for me is the Objectivist philosophy of Ayn Rand, in particular her revolutionary thinking in the field of ethics. I borrowed the salute, "To a life, which is a reason unto itself" from Rand's first big novel, *We the Living*. To Maria Montessori, Lisa Van Damme, and like-minded philosophers of education, my character, Alek Rankl, would tip his hat, as do I. Lenore Pellon is the fictional stand-in for my first philosophy professor, Leonard Peikoff. The classroom scene of Lenore Pellon and the sneering student who makes bold to

Acknowledgements

question Aristotle's law of contradiction is just about verbatim a scene I witnessed in a Leonard Peikoff logic class at the long-ago Polytechnic Institute of Brooklyn.

For purely literary influences, thank you, James Clavell, for the security agent in *Noble House* who "watched without watching" and for the marvelous metaphor of "pillowing" in *Shogun*. And thank you, Walt Whitman, for the man whom people "wish long and long to be with," in his exultant poem, "I Sing the Body Electric." I use these words to refer to Marek Rankl and suspect old Walt had himself in mind when he wrote them.

In the category of inspirational influences, my gratitude goes to Thomas Paine and America's other founding giants. You dared to begin the world over again, battled to pull it off, and then designed a government to make it a reality. Thank you Rachmaninoff, Chopin, and Martha Argerich for inspiration lavishly provided during the most difficult chapters of this book, and Jerrold Meyer, for reading four preview chapters. Your enthusiastic feedback buoyed me at a time when I truly needed it. Thank you, Alexandra York, whose powerful first novel, *Crosspoints*, dared me to venture into the daunting realm of novel writing. And to my beloved Judith Stewart who is my Emma Lane, whose quiet flame is always there for me, my undying gratitude for the private Arête we share in our life together.

And finally, on top of his editing genius, Alex Bleier, my closest friend, was and is a constant inspiration due to the radiant inner flame which is so uniquely his own. Together, we pursued the vision of Arête set forth in this book. And on the journey, we found that we were already there.

It is a most excellent place.

***

Printed in Great Britain
by Amazon